CIVIL WAR
WOMEN II

CIVIL WAR WOMEN II

Stories by Women about Women

Edited by Martin H. Greenberg,
Charles G. Waugh, and
Frank D. McSherry, Jr.

With an introduction
by Catherine Clinton

August House Publishers, Inc.
LITTLE ROCK

Published 1997 by August House, Inc.,
P.O. Box 3223, Little Rock, Arkansas, 72203,
501-372-5450.

Printed in the United States of America
10 9 8 7 6 5 4 3 2 1

LIBRARY OF CONGRESS CATALOGING-IN-PUBLICATION DATA

Civil War women II: stories by women about women/ edited by Martin H. Greenberg,
Charles G. Waugh, and Frank D. McSherry, Jr.; with an introduction by Catherine
Clinton.
p. cm.
Contents: My Thanksgiving / Rose Terry Cooke—Margaret Bronson / Elizabeth Stuart
Phelps Ward—The lamp of Psyche / Edith Wharton—Brave Mrs. Lyle / Sarah B.
Cooper—From a soldier's wife / Bella Z. Spencer—Mary Bowman / Elsie Singmaster—
The blue and the grey / Louisa May Alcott—The last of seven /
Louise C. Moulton.
ISBN 0-87483-487-2
1. United States—History—Civil War, 1861-1865—Women—Fiction.
2. United States—History—Civil War, 1861-1865—Fiction. 3. Short stories, American—
Women authors. 4. War stories, American.
I. Greenberg, Martin Harry. II. Waugh, Charles. III. McSherry, Frank D.
IV. Title: Civil War women 2. V. Title: Civil War women Two.
PS648.C54C536   1997
813'.0108358—DC21   97-7105

President and publisher: Ted Parkhurst
Executive editor: Liz Parkhurst
Project editor: Suzi Parker
Cover design: Byron Taylor

AUGUST HOUSE, INC.   PUBLISHERS   LITTLE ROCK

WOMAN'S PART IN WAR

Mary H. Southworth Kimbrough

Who bears the long suspense of war? Who pays
With tears the cannon's cost? Who must behold
The maimèd forms of those brave sons she bore
When from the bloody battle field they bring
Them home? And who must comfort, who restore
Men's shattered hopes—who must extract the sting
When victory has passed them by? . . . We know
Whose task this is. Since first the world began,
It has been woman's part in war. 'Twas so
When Southland's bugles called, and tidings ran
Of Southland's jeopardy from end to end
Of our fair land. Our mothers heard and wept,
Then kissed their sons and sent them to defend
Their righteous cause. And every warrior kept
Within his heart his pledge to one brave saint
To match her sacrifice with noble deed.

O great Confederate mothers, we would paint
Your names on monuments, that men may read
Them as the years go by and tribute pay
To you who bore and nurtured hero-sons
And gave them solace on that darkest day
When they came home with broken swords and guns!

CONTENTS

INTRODUCTION

ᚖ

It has been doubly rewarding to prepare an introduction for *Civil War Women II*. First and foremost, I am pleased to see the crowded crossroads where popular interest in the American Civil War and the flourishing of women's studies intersect. Second, being introduced to the following stories renews my faith in the powers and pathos of the Civil War not only to reshape an era, but to incalculably redefine future generations—to remind us of our lasting connections to this unfolding story. As sagas of the Civil War are endlessly recovered and rediscovered within our history and literature, they continue vibrant and meaningful for us during the 1990s as much as they were for Americans during the 1890s.

With this sequel to their successful first volume, the editors have provided us with a title, *Civil War Women II*, which offers *double entendres*. The title reminds us "women, *too*" for scholars in the trenches of Civil War Studies and, don't forget, "*Civil War* women, too!" for scholars laboring in the vineyards of American women's history. These ironic reminders are luckily less necessary than they might have been only a decade ago.

In addition, the stories of the first volume offered such quality that the appetite of readers was whetted for this second installment, which will doubtless stimulate further interest. Our hunger seems insatiable, and treasures remarkably remain buried within our literary heritage, as this exciting octet of heroine indicate.

From the wartime publication of Louisa May Alcott, to a story from Edith Wharton, this volume provides a rich cross-section of women's postwar writing. This collected work reflects the depth wartime experience afforded both women and men for generations. Even more significantly, they provide an embellishment of our usual images of war. Not all battles were waged on the front. From empty hearthsides to hospital wards, from isolated Indiana farmsteads to a little shop on the Rue Bonaparte in Paris, these fictional memoirs take us on sentimental and sobering journeys, revisiting war's incredible, indelible impact.

In all of these stories, women authors create heroines whose steadfast fortitude, whose faith and sacrifice are the backbone of their communities—long after war's end. The northern heroine in "My Thanksgiving" by Rose Terry Cooke (1886) feels a kinship with her southern sisters, and confesses in the wake of battle deaths "we could hold open arms to rebel women, and weep with them in the divine reconciliation of a mutual sorrow." These women's sacrifices are a common thread throughout all the stories. The only theme that surpasses is, not surprisingly, the monolith of female patriotism, which rarely transcends strong nationalist and sectionalist divides.

From Cooke's first story onward, these women are ardent supporters of their men's decision to enlist (with the exception of one Quaker dissenter). Women all rally to the cause of their country—whatever the consequences. In the case of Cooke's heroine, Ann, she sends forth her fiance Joe, although she only quite recently realized he was the love of her life. Despite the dramatic circumstances, she releases him without reproach.

Each and every woman did not just accept the inevitable, but embraced the tenet of faith that lovers and husbands, fathers and brothers march off to battle. Ann's sweetheart reminds her to not forget to celebrate Thanksgiving, to keep Christmas. She overcomes her sense of mourning, once he is lost in battle, and is rewarded for her devotion to her duty. The twists of fate that Cooke allows, and a woman's faith keeps love (and lover) alive.

In the second selection, we are introduced to an even more complex romantic heroine, with Elizabeth Stuart Phelps Ward's "Margaret Bronson." Bronson was a "young woman who carried pistols, had no desire to marry, and was not afraid of guerrillas." War provides us with a popular postwar literary cliche, as Bronson was a "good Southerner" who freed her slaves. But this story does not dwell on sectional politics, and anti-slavery, but is a rip-roaring adventure full of secret rendez-vous and disguised loyalties. The unspoken love between Margaret Bronson and Robert M'Ginley reveals itself during the heat of battle, and—at long last—Ward's heroine finds her match, and, perhaps even a mate.

One of the most intriguing tales of the collection is from the pen of Edith Wharton, "The Lamp of Psyche," which appeared in *Scribner's* in 1895, one of her earliest publications. It is only one of two pieces of Wharton's fiction where she deals explicitly with the Civil War, despite her deep and abiding interest in the era, demonstrated by voracious consumption of volumes of Civil War history.

Perhaps the tale is more autobiographical than Wharton would have liked: her story, so damning of those who "sat out" the war, and her father without any military service. Indeed, Wharton refused to allow Edward Burlingame, the editor of *Scribner's*, to include this piece in her first collection of short stories, *The Greater Inclination* (1899), despite his persistent requests.

As the story opens, Delia Corbett is blissful. Wharton reports: "To her had been given the one portion denied to all other women on earth, the immense, the unapproachable privilege of becoming Laurence Corbett's wife." This triumph is even sweeter as "she was past thirty," her first marriage had been unhappy, and she had remarried Corbett as a widow.

The couple live a completely idyllic life in Europe until they return to Boston to visit Delia's Aunt Mary, who casually inquires about Corbett when she has Delia alone: "Then, of course he was in the war...You've never told me about that. Did he see active service?"

Delia is forced to recall what she had perhaps repressed: "All the men of her family, all the men of her friends' families, had fought in the war; Mrs. Hayne's [Aunt Mary's] husband had been killed at Bull Run, and one of Delia's cousins at Gettysburg. Ever since she could remember it had been regarded as a matter of course by those about her that every man of her husband's generation who was neither lame, halt, not blind should have fought in the war." Despite the rising tide of feeling with Delia, she replies coldly: "I really don't know. I never asked him."

The torment and outcome of this incident is Wharton at her best. The couple returns to Paris with Delia's "increasing fear of her aunt's unspoken verdict." The hope against hope is shattered, just like the crystal on a miniature portrait Corbett buys his wife in a shop on the Rue Bonaparte, with its inscription on the back "Fell at Chancellorsville, May 3, 1863." Delia finally confronts her husband about his "reasons for remaining at home," and their relationship is forever changed. Wharton is powerfully sardonic, her understatement is overpowering within this tale of love transformed.

Sarah B. Cooper's "Brave Mrs. Lyle" (1873) provides an equally strong tale of love and its consequences. Her language is perhaps the most colorful within the volume, full of wartime voices, describing "a catawamtious old cuss...too big for his boots" who "flipfloppussed himself before he knows it."

Her protagonist, the heroic Eunice Lyle, is an equally colorful "Mother Courage," forced to ride through rainstorms, rescue people from burned-out houses, bury a neighbor's wife, and care for her orphaned children, as she loses two of her own offspring and is forced to become a refugee. But even as her family suffers loss and dislocation, she is willing to part with her beloved oldest son, Charlie, and send him off to military school, in case his country needs his service.

In Belle Spencer's "A Soldier's Wife," the author takes the reader through the step-by-step loss of innocence suffered by her heroine. This morality tale again offers women during wartime, as her story appeared in June 1864, a sense of redemption, that their faith and courage will not only sustain themselves, but have an important impact on the soldiers they send off to war, and the war itself. Spencer explains her heroine's learning "to think less of myself and more of others," and then takes us through the process. She toils ceaselessly in the sick ward, and exhausted contemplates taking "an hour's rest," but worries that her charge might die and "could (she) feel that I did all in my power to save him? Not if I should yield to the inclination I felt to abandon my post; so I remained and tried to be patient." She learns impatience as well, when her husband is missing and reported dead after a battle. Spencer's heroine at first "sank slowly into utter oblivion," but then demands to be taken to the front to find him, and prevails against advice and the odds, to seek him out—sailing alone by riverboat, then tromping through a sea of mud, then searching the blood-stained battlefield, not taking no for an answer. Her faith is repaid by a miracle, and she is reunited with her husband.

Not all women were so fortunate. Elsie Singmaster's "Mary Bowman" offers a gripping image of war: a woman rocking on her porch-front at Gettysburg, fifty years after she lost her husband who was buried among the unknown dead. She looks out over the monuments at sunset, as "marble shafts and domes turn to liquid gold." We share her painful memories as she hears "the pouring rain of July the fourth, falling upon her little house, upon the wide battle-field upon her very heart." Bowman waits patiently, a product of love and Christian faith, biding her time until she is reunited.

Faith plays an equally compelling role in Louisa May Alcott's "The Blue and the Gray" (1868), when a saintly nurse, Miss Mercy, witnesses (or engineers) the redemptive power of religion. The guilt of a dying rebel soldier, sickened by his role in the death of his Yankee roommate, causes him to suffer remorse, to try to right a wrong. The intricate interplay of hate and intrigue, suffering and sharing unfold in Alcott's sentimental tale. The power of faith, the rule of "Mercy" in the wards and in the war, is meant to comfort those who lost loved ones. Alcott reminds readers that not all wartime drama was confined to the battlefield.

And finally, Louise Moulton's "The Last of Seven" tells the story of a daughter who not only reclaims her love from the jaws of death, but through her pure and spiritual devotion to her soldier, she renews her parents' love for one another. It is a very tangled and complex drama, dwelling on the magical prospects of a seventh child, Winnie Gibson, and this daughter's devotion to her soldier, James Ransom. But in other ways, Moulton retells a simple story—a wartime "Romeo and Juliet" with a happy rather than tragic outcome.

Moulton perhaps uses names to add symbolic punch to her tale. The payment of "Ransom's" life is the price that reveals to Adam Gibson the error of his patriarchal rule. And Moulton was perhaps well aware that by naming her heroine Winnie, parallels with a popular postwar romantic tragedy might be drawn. Varina Davis, the youngest daughter of Jefferson Davis, born in 1864, was nicknamed Winnie. She spent most of her early years aboard yet became known as "The Daughter of the Confederacy." Winnie fulfilled her duty by dedicating memorials, addressing veterans, becoming a living symbol of Confederate memorialization. In the 1880s when she fell in love with Yankee Alfred Wilkinson, Jr., the grandson of an abolitionist, the outcry was so strong, that her engagement was broken off. Winnie never married and it was romantically alleged she eventually died "of a broken heart."

There were dozens such postwar melodramas, and Moulton and others bring these folktales and romances to bear as well as the stand (and remarkable) tales of deserters, refugees, renegades, and pistol-packing women. At the same time the editors of *Civil War Women II* have taken pains to find us heroines who both define and defy cliche—stoic Mrs. Bowman, vibrant Miss Mercy, intrepid Mrs. Lyle, saintly Mrs. S—, defeated Delia Corbett, and ennobled Margaret Bronson, as well as the devoted fianceés: Ann, who opens the books, and Winnie, who closes the volume. Although these surface and resurface again, although surprising twists of fate reappear with remarkable frequency, each author stamps her story with the imprint of an unforgettable heroine. This enthralling cast of characters will draw you further, and with pleasure, into *Civil War Women II*.

Catherine Clinton
Riverside, Connecticut

My Thanksgiving

Rose Terry Cooke

I must go, Annie! said Joe, speaking with a calm resolution that I felt to be final and fatal; all the more so that he put his arm round me as he spoke, and drew me to him in a clasp so close that it said more than words. Granny looked up from the chimney-corner where she sat, and said, in her feeble voice and deliberate accent:—

"Who died for us!"

These few words, so seemingly irrelevant, but merely seeming so because they drew a deeper significance than from the shallow present alone, smote on my ear like a knell. I looked up into Joe's face as it bent over me, brown and stern and sad, and as I looked, with all my life in the gaze, a cold shadow stole across that living countenance: it grew cold, rigid, ghastly; the mouth parted over its set teeth; the eyelids closed; it was a dead face. I involuntarily uttered a little shriek; and then for one second heard a word breathed through Joe's lips, and knew that he was not dead, but praying.

"What is it, Annie?" said he, gently.

"Oh Joe! I cannot, cannot bear it!"

"My child, you must. This is no time for a man to be at home, no time for a woman to be a coward. You must not make me weak, or send me away lonely; for I should be doubly alone if I thought my—my wife,

Annie, could not strike hand with me in this good cause."

The words breathed a steady glow of strength into me. I saw what I ought to do, what I must do for him; and from its broken deeps in my breaking heart the old puritan blood that trickled from Winslow's veins down through mine answered to the appeal, and fired my brain and steadied my voice with its firm pulses. I pulled Joe's dark head down to mine and kissed his lips. I was not his wife yet,—perhaps now I never should be; but heart and soul we were indissolubly bound, and I had a right to kiss him without blushes or trembling. Hard, hard it was! Myriads of us all over this struggling, bleeding country know how hard; and know that even at this deadly crises we could hold open arms to rebel women, and weep with them in the divine reconciliation of a mutual sorrow. Harder it was to me because, just now, I knew for the first time how utterly I loved Joe; and to tell why, I must go back a little into my past.

Granny Harding, who sat there in the fireplace corner, was Joe's great-grandmother as well as mine, though we were not even third cousins for all that. Joe's grandfather was her own son, my grandmother was her step-daughter; the relationship was scarce worth mentioning, nor would it have been recorded, unless in the big Bible, except that all the Harding race had always lived and died in Stoneboro. My grandmother was the parson's wife there; my father succeeded his father in the office, and was called "the minister" instead of the "the parson." Father and mother both died when I was nine years old, and Cousin Aristarchus Harding, Joe's father, was my guardian. So I went to his house—the old Harding homestead—to live, and found there Joe, three years older than I, and Cordelia, of my own age.

Probably the reason I had never fallen in love, as girls say, with Joe was because I lived in the same house with him. He was always kind, and good, and considerate; but I was romantic, and in some respects a fool. I could not hang my ideal lover on the aspect of a young man I saw eating and drinking, and mowing, and splitting wood, and making fires, and driving oxen; a man in his shirt-sleeves and an old hat. It was impossible to find a sentimental and high-flown interest, such as Thaddeus of Warsaw would have excited, in an ordinary farmer, who only did his duty from day to day, and never talked about congeniality of soul or magnetic sympathies. Joe was not so hard to please; he began to love me very early; everything I did was right and pleasant in his eyes. I suited him exactly. My sauciness bewitched him; my prettiness, such as it was, pleased his taste. I always knew what he thought, and understood what he meant to say when he could not express it. I liked the things he liked, and I teased his monotonous farm-life into vitality. I was his romance; and it cruelly smote Joe when I fell in love with—somebody else!

Why, in the name of common-sense, when I had beside me this true, generous, gentle man, who was as much devoted to me as a man can be, I threw myself away on a hard, cool, selfish, imperious nature that only gave me the careless affection one bestows on a pretty child they have no time to love, Heaven only knows! It is a part of the mysteries we live in, that women have done, do, and will do so till time shall be no more; and there must be some good purpose of compensation or discipline in it; but it is a deadly experience, and where it is not mortal leaves frightful scars on heart and mind. I am inclined to think those whose ties of this kind culminate in marriage suffer more than those who escape before it; in either case it is bad enough. I was eighteen when I met this man, whose name I have no desire to recall; ten of my life's best years he wasted. In those ten years I loved him with the eager, faithful passion of youth and womanhood, grew slowly to know him, ruminated over this bitter herb of knowledge till my life was burnt with its acrid essence into pale ashes. For five years he made love to me, taught me to love, to doubt, to dread him; then, tired of his toy, he left me and Stoneboro, and for five years more I was broken in health and spirit down to the very dust. People in Stoneboro said I was "disappointed." So I was.

In the meantime Cordelia married and moved away. I did not miss her particularly. She was a good, placid, amiable creature, mildly pious and very common-place. I should have loved her better if I had not been absorbed in my own affairs. The first thing that roused me from my self-absorbed misery was Cousin Martha Harding's falling into a severe illness. If I loved anybody then better than myself, which I doubt, it was Cousin Martha. She was the sweetest of sweet women; not with the super-saccharine manner of fashion and society,—no more like that suave and popular sweetness than maple-sugar is like Maillard's confectionery; but her nature was as fragrant and satisfying as wild honey. The homely flavor of a New England farm-life touched all she said with a certain quaintness, and her serene, but trenchant, common-sense and acute insight kept her unfailing good-nature from insipidity. She was quite deaf; a loss which added to her manner the exquisite gentleness rarely found except in the deaf, and very rarely among them; for it takes, as old Parson Winslow, my grandfather, used to say, "grace and gifts too" to bear such a deprivation with patience till it blossoms into a beauty. And this lovely, loving woman, who had been my mother in a certain imperfect sense, fell into a wasting consumption; and when I knew it I put aside my long repining, or rather it crept away before the face of so vital and inevitable a sorrow.

But all this long time Joe, though I did not see it, had watched me with the tenderest care,—his heart had been scarce less wrung with my trouble than my own,—but had given no sign to vex me. He had been my protector against rude tongues and the pangs that careless ones can inflict. He had tried with all his might to allay my physical suffering, and patiently striven to heal my mind; but in vain. I had adopted fully the girl's idea that constancy is a virtue instead of a fact; and long after I knew thoroughly how ill-placed my love had been, what sure and life-long misery I had lost in losing that love, I still clung to its ghost with dreary strenuousness, cherished its memory, dwelt on its frail souvenirs, recalled its raptures, and spent sleepless nights and long days in persuading myself that my heart was dead in my breast, that I had loved once for all, and lived my life out. All this Joe saw; but, with a fidelity that shamed my pretense to it, he really loved me still. He did not grieve, or fret, or give up his time and health, but, like the true man he was, only threw himself into harder work, and fed his self-denying love with such considerate care, such tender though, such unflagging service for me, that he was almost happy in his pure self-devotion.

He grew gray, it is true, in those ten years; his dark curls were full of silver threads; the gay, bright face, scarce handsome, but full of intellect, and as gracious as summer in its smile, was thinner than it should have been, deep-lined about its grave lips, and serious even to sadness; but he went about his life's business so earnestly, with such energy and cheer,— was so helpful to everybody, so kind, so strong,—that nobody knew what he felt, or how he suffered, but Cousin Martha. To her he told every thought of his heart; and it was the very bitterness of death to Joe, when he at length was forced to see that mortal disease had fastened on that mother, dearer even than I.

Three long years life flashed and faded, and flashed again, in that racked frame, till it could bear no longer those terrible alterations. Consumption has in it a certain practical sarcasm that is hard to bear; it makes a mock of weakness with its sudden, but false, strength; it fires the eye, and paints the cheek, and sends vivid fever through the leaping pulse, till immortal youth and strength seem to defy death, and riot in their splendors; then comes the recoil of mortal weakness, a sunken cheek, a colorless lip, a dim and glazing eye, coughs that rend the panting breast, pains like the torture of rack and wheel in every wasted limb, the dreadful gush of scarlet blood, utter prostration of arterial life, the passive sinking of nerve, and excitement of brain; and then again, reeling from the very abyss of death, the tormented prey of this vulture rises to life, blooms, brightens, exults, till another hour turns the descending scale. Three long years Joe and I watched and waited together. Cordelia was in Minnesota with a flock of little children, and we had Cousin Martha all to ourselves; for granny was now ninety-three, and could not help us, except that she was able, with very little aid, to take care of herself. And Cousin Aristarchus was no help; his great, slow-beating heart knew but one intense passion, and that was for his wife, and now he suffered accordingly. He would come into the room where she lay, stand and look at her with such an expression in his rough face, reddened with summer sun and winter frost through fifty-five years of a farmer's hardships, that I could not look at him. It was a dull, uncomprehending anguish at first, like the look of an animal in mortal pain; but deepening, as days went on, into the extremity of human suffering, heightened by wild conflict with the inevitable Will that could alone save, but offered here neither help nor hope. If she opened her large, languid eyes to look at him, or smiled, as she could sometimes smile, with a look that was almost supernatural in its triumph of love, pity, and patience over the extremity of pain, he turned at once and went away—where, nobody knew. I happened once to be in the barn, looking for a fresh egg, when he rushed by, without seeing me at all, and, flinging himself at length on the hay, groaned, and sobbed, and writhed, and cried out so bitterly, that it was terrible to see or hear. I crept away silently, awed and sick at heart. I had not supposed such feeling was possible in a man. I had judged them all with warped judgment, from the one I knew best. I had no faith in them; but this was real. What could life offer to a woman better than such a mighty love as this? My unconscious egotism prompted one little question: would Joe ever love like his father?

So, as I said, Mr. Harding could not share our care; he felt too much, and no discipline of life had every taught him self-control. But we had no need of aid. Joe was one of those rare men who have a woman's perception as well as a man's strength, and with his aid Cousin Martha needed no other nurse than me.

At last she kept her bed; she could not sit up even for an hour; but still her cheerful voice, her unselfish regard for our strength and comfort, her patience in pain, her upholding religion, triumphed over these terrors and pangs of mortality. I could not understand her. To die; to be exiled forever from this body and this dear earth; to tempt an utterly untried existence, to lose that locality of place and time that the trembling soul lays hold of when it shudders at its own eternity and infinite capacities; to enter the cold newness of another world, austere from its very strangeness, with such simple courage, such certainty, such calm faith,—surprised me all the time; it seemed incredible. But Joe also partook of this vital belief. He talked calmly of that near and unseen world, and of his mother's passage thither. In the midst of his tenderest cares he had lips overflowing with the trumpet-blasts of the gospel; his face kindled with victory, his voice thrilled with assurance for her, even while the depth of settled sorrow in his eye showed no stir, no spark, it was for himself he had to grieve, and he forgot himself; for her he was triumphant. If I had stopped to look into my own heart I should have seen how effectually it was laying hold upon another love, as different from my first as the yellow wheat ear is from the springing blade.

But while day after day I drew nearer to Joe in the feeling, and regarded him with such a quiet sense of safety and repose, I did not, could not, stop to dream of love. I was learning a new lesson,—learning to believe. The feeble emotional pretext I had called religion, and professed as such, that had crumbled away in the convulsive grasp of sorrow and left me unsupported, was being gradually replaced by a living faith. Blessed is the woman who loves a man better than she is! It is not often so; but it is the sure sea of that marriage that God ordained, and typified by his love for the Church, when King and Priest reign and minister in the sacred cloisters of home, and give themselves, even as he gave himself, for the love and teaching of the weaker. I did not know where I was, till one day, about a month before Cousin Martha died, I observed her look follow Joe wistfully out of the room, and then turn to me with a curious expression of regret and longing. Involuntarily I said:—

"What is it, dear?"

"Come here, Annie," said she. So I went and kneeled down by the bedside.

"I want to tell you something, my child; Joe loves you dearly."

"O cousin, you don't know! He doesn't; how could he?"

"But he does; and has for this fourteen years."

"Love me! I am not fit for Joe to love."

"Annie, I don't believe dying wishes are more to be regarded than living ones; they are all liable to be short-sighted and selfish. You must promise not to feel bound by any desire of mine; but I must tell you how happy it would make me if you could love Joe enough to marry him."

I buried my head in my hands. "Cousin Martha, you *are* mistaken. Joe doesn't love me; think how old I am,—I was thirty last spring,—and how homely I am, and not good either; and—and, besides, I have loved somebody else."

A smile just glittered wanly in her eyes, and she laid her hand on my hair, as I looked up at her with a burning face. "Poor child!" said she. "I know how you have suffered, though I never said so to you. Those things are best kept silent. But Joe is a better man than that one; and he loves you better; believe it, for I know it. And now we will let the matter rest."

"God is good!" said granny. She had a strange way of coming out with apparently irrelevant bits of Scripture, or odd proverbs, or sayings of her own, at times when no one supposed she heard or saw what was going on, as she seemed sunk in her habitual revery.

"Yes, he is!" said Cousin Martha.

I think I said so, too, mentally, as I got up and went out of doors into the little bit of woods that sloped up the hill-side behind the barn, where I sat down under a great oak-tree through whose gnarled boughs, just roughened with buds, the March sunshine streamed strangely warm. I could not believe it! Was I in love again? Was this strong torrent of emotion a new fishnet in the stream that had wrecked me before? Did I love Joe Harding? I'm afraid I did, even then. I recognized with a certain pang the old rush of feeling, yet not now the vague, feverish emotion that had wrapped my whole nature in a light blaze before; but a deeper, steadier fire, that rose heavenward with solemn aspiration as from an altar, and promised to be life-giving instead of deadly. I ought, perhaps, to be sorry to confess that I did not stop to regret my beautiful theory of constancy; I never was a very introspective person. The thing was gone, and there was an end of it for me. The theory had disproved itself, and so was negatived; that was only another fact. I found time afterward to be heartily glad that I could love again, and so much more deeply. This unutterable rest, this serene rapture, one hour of which was worth a year of the excitement and restless wearing delight of my youth, was certainly a thing to be glad of, unless one had been more or less than a woman.

One thing struck me to the heart whenever I dared look that way: the possibility that Joe might not love me, after all; that Cousin Martha was mistaken. It seemed so impossible. My youth was gone, my beauty faded, my vivacity all fled; I had been made the sport of another man, and thrown away by him when he tired. Was there in humanity such redeeming love as could stoop to gather this week of my life and wear it for a cognizance? I should as soon think of giving to a lover some wan and withered rose picked up from the pavement, without beauty of freshness, as the worthless gift I was. Cousin Martha must be mistaken. How could he love me? Before, and of that other, I had said so many times with hot and salt tears, "How could he help loving me?"

I went back to my room and looked into the glass; a new bloom shone on the old face, but did not transfigure it. There were the pale, worn features; the sad eyes; the bands of hair still shining, but all threaded with snow; the lightly tinted lips that were so tremulous and grieving now, instead of smiling and firm. I was old: I turned away with a sigh from that vision. Men do not love beauty more than women, only they are more frank to own it; and to lose mine, which was always that of color and outline rather than feature, was hard.

Cousin Martha grew worse that night, and kept worse. No more respites for her; the hour came fast that should take her from us, and, except as a thought that I kept to rest myself with at intervals of watching and nursing, I heard and knew no more of Joe's love for me.

At length she died, not with any parting word or message, not with any scene; but fell asleep like a tired child, holding her husband's hand. There was no need of audible triumph in her testimony; her life was her witness, and they who had seen its quiet course knew from what source it sprung, to what glad sea it hastened. Joe and I also sat beside her, and when we saw that it was over he gently lifted her hand from his father's clasp and laid it back at her side. Mr. Harding looked up with dreadful questioning in his eyes, and then looked at her. He went out of the door and out of the house, and for hours we saw him no more. Joe would not let him be looked for, and at sunset he reappeared. He never said anything, but from that day was a broken man; his grizzled hair turned white, his keen eye was dimmed, his voice husky; even the rugged and set features learned to quiver with passing emotions; the firm temper became fitful; he asked help that he laughed at before; he clung to those about him in little ways hitherto unknown to him. I never loved him as much. Granny looked at Cousin Martha's pallid, but fair, aspect, and took the wasted hand in hers: she did not moan nor weep; all she said was, "Behold how He loved him!"

There was no other change than this inevitable change of loss. The fire seemed to have gone out of our lives, the light to be extinguished, it is true; but the household ways went on as usual, for I had taken charge of them long before, and now they were my sole occupation.

One day in May, when all the trees were full of opal tints, pink, or green, or dusky with young buds, and even the oaks put out tiny velvet leaves of tender pink from the heart of every new shoot, Joe asked me to go to the graveyard with him; and when we had planted by his mother's grave a rose-bush and some English violets, we strolled away into the woods and sat down on a log. Below us lay the Stoneboro valley, with its bright river sparkling in and out among the hills, and a soft south wind blew on us with odors of dead and new leaves, the fresh scent of grass, and breath of orchards in bloom. We sat a long time in silence, and then Joe said:—

"Annie, can you possible love me enough?"

"I'll try," said I, with half a laugh, though I could hardly speak at all.

He put his arm round me and kissed me gravely, and that was all we said. I felt so safe, so rested, so consoled. I did not want words, and he seemed not to have them. I forgot how old and plain and undeserving I was: I ought to have refused him for his own good, but I couldn't. I was not very good, and I was so glad he loved me.

When we went home there was a little blaze kindled on the kitchen hearth; we sat there in winter and spring always, for it was never used as a kitchen, and granny's bedroom opened out of it. To-night she sat there in the flicker of the blaze, knitting placidly as usual. Her delicate, pale face; her soft hair, white as milk-weed down; her light gray dress and full-folded white cap, handkerchief, and linen apron gave her the look of a white moth, such as peers in through the window on some June night, with elfin visage and bright, dark eyes. She looked up as we came in, and gazed intently at us for a minute, then nodded with a satisfied air, and said, "Fulfilling of the law."

Joe smiled, and I believe I blushed; next morning Cousin Aristarchus, when I came down to breakfast, came and shook hands with me, and looked the other way all the time. It was all he could do, and a great effort for him; so I accepted it as a congratulation and welcome. It was about three weeks after this that Joe came in and told me he had enlisted and was going to the war, as I said in the beginning of my story. He had longed to go all the time but could not think it right to leave his mother, especially as she begged him to stay with her while she lived. Now, when rebellion was higher-handed than ever, the army of the Peninsula in deadly straits, the West in terror, and two new calls proclaimed by the President, go he must. Now was the time for men, if ever.

I had to consent, of course. I am not a heroic woman. I was not glad to have him go, yet I should have been thoroughly ashamed had he stayed; doubly ashamed to have felt afterward that, even at the saving of his life, he had deserted his country at need. No. Unhappy enough are those women who lose their dearest in battle, though they fight and fall in the good cause; but wretched, far beyond any loss, are they whose unwomanly fears keep from the country's service men she needs—who must say to their children afterward, answering their child-questions, "Your father did not go to the war, I would not let him."

No such fate for me. Dear as Joe was to me, dearer every day,—far more dear than I thought any living creature could ever be,—I choked down my agonies of foreboding, and let him go. In this my sole comfort was preparing his outfit. Granny knit him more stockings than he could take, and every little contrivance that might add to his comfort I took pride in discovering and procuring. He enlisted as private in a company of the Sixteenth Connecticut Volunteers, which in August went into camp at Hartford. Once he came home to Stoneboro for a three-days' furlough, and we had one talk that I shall never forget.

"Annie," said he, "I want you to promise me something. I know how you will miss me, and how hard a time you will have; but promise you will not let your grief interfere with the usual routine of home. I don't mean simply on granny's account and father's, but on your own. Keep up all the old ways, for the sake of your own quiet. Don't let the farm go back because I'm not here; father will feel more interest in it if you are interested. Go to church, and to singing-meeting, and to sewing-society; wherever I am, dead or alive, don't omit to keep Thanksgiving; don't forget Christmas; and the poor—you know you have them always with you, He said."

"I will, Joe, if I can."

"You can, dear, if you begin straight. Habit is a great help, and in this quiet little village there is no excitement to divert your mind, which you must keep as firm and calm as you can; for, Annie,—you must look it in the face,—it is very probable I may not come back, and these old people will only have you left."

There was no answer to be made to this. The next day Joe bade us good-by and went off. We heard from him twice before they left Hartford; he was well and gravely cheerful.

As for me, there was but one course left,— I must work. No other quiet but that of constant action and effort could allay the dreadful fever of my thoughts. I was naturally both anxious and imaginative,—fatal combination for a woman whose place is to wait and endure! So by day I worked as I never had before. I let the girl whose place it was to take care of the milk, butter, and cheese, go home to her mother, as she had long intended to do at this time, without trying to supply her place. I could do her work, as far as skill went, better than she, and the constant excitement of anxiety made me strong. I had to rise early, and work hard; labor of real and stringent grasp held me all day; from dawn till blank night I was busy. There was the milk of twelve cows to strain, and set, and skim; the milk-room, and the cheese-room, and the ice-cellar to be kept spotless and of just temperature; there were rows of cheeses, pressing, ripening, drying, to be looked at twice a day; there was curd to set, and cut, and drain, and salt; moulds to be scoured, cloths to be scalded; daily the great churn, that a man had to turn, yielded me its crumbly mass of yellow butter, to be worked, salted, moulded, and packed for market,—butter that must be firm and sweet, hard as wax, and gold-yellow, lest our farm should lose its reputation for the best butter sent to Boston. Then came numberless pans, and cream-jars, and butter-pails to wash: these never passed out of my hands, lest the careless eyes of a servant might leave some grain of milk, some smear of cream, that should turn sour and spoil my work. Besides these things there was granny to care for; she needed some help to dress her in those quaint white folds and frills that she delighted to wear; help she needed, too, in order to lay them aside, and put herself into sleeping order,—for never by any chance was the delicately stiff cap permitted to rest by day against a chair-back, or the folds of cambric that covered her breast ruffled by one minute of repose out of position: if she slept by day, it was bolt upright, as she sat. The last thing at night was work too: the night's milk was to be strained and set; that of the night before must be skimmed, and the emptied pans scalded and dried; by nine o'clock I was so tired out that sleep caught me without my knowing it, and in dreamless exhaustion I knew nothing till the noisy fowls in the poultry-yard woke me to dawn and its necessary duties. Yet not all this work and weariness kept my eager, restless thoughts from Joe. They followed him, invisible, yet faithful, courier, on every step of his journey,—into camp, at drill; farther I knew not,—till in so short a time after he left Hartford that it seemed to me scarce the lapse of three days, though I knew it was more, the news of Antietam struck us like a bolt from the clear sky.

I did not believe it when Cousin Aristarchus told me. I laughed.

"Why," said I, "it is impossible. The Sixteenth hadn't their arms, they were but just there; they could not have been sent into a battle."

"They were," said he, turning his keen gray eyes away from me, and dropping his white head slowly, as if it were heavy with some heavy grief. My heart fell.

"Is there any definite news?—any list of dead or wounded, cousin?" said I, the words faltering, as I spoke.

"No," said he. "The news came to Hartford yesterday morning, or Saturday night,—I don't know which. There was news of one officer killed; no particulars further."

He stopped, and looked aside out of the window; he had not finished. I waited breathless for the next words.

"No," he said, at length, drawing a long breath, and saying over, as if it were a lesson, the very words, I was sure, he had seen on the bulletin at the post-office; "Nothing definite as to names; the Sixteenth cut to pieces."

I sat down in the nearest chair, and he walked out of the kitchen. Grief never comes so, there is a shock, a paralysis, a shuddering novelty, but not grief. I sat there still as the dread grasp that stiffens every fibre holds the paralytic. I could not stir, because I forgot how. I was lost in one great spasm of resistance, of repulsion. I did not, would not, believe anything had come to Joe. Presently sense and strength returned to me. What a fool I was! I had heard nothing, knew nothing. Why should not Joe be saved as well as any other man? I tried to laugh, as one does sometimes in a dark room waking from fearful dreams, to reassure himself, but the old kitchen walls seemed to make a hollow echo of my forced mirth; or was it hollow of itself? Granny came out of her room, tottering on the cane that Joe had wrought and ornamented for her.

"Crackling thorns!" said she, lifting up her white head and looking vacantly before her. A cold shiver ran over me. I am superstitious, like all women; and granny's words, quaint and irrelevant as they seemed to others, I had a sort of reverence for that gave them prophetic significance in my eyes. Yes, my laughter was crackling thorns indeed! The fire was of briers that rankled in my grasp still; the flame but one flash, vivid and noisy, that quivered, flared, fell into ashes.

I helped her to her chair, and turned into the cheese-room for my work, sick at heart. There is a strange balsamic power in routine, when the very depths of life break up under your feet; the daily order of occupation is a light, but tenacious, crust above those volcanic surges; and though you feel their sickening undulations, and hear their threatening roar beneath, yet the gulf does not open and swallow you up,—the thunder is muffled, the fires smoulder. There is a place for human feet to tread, a point for the lever of divine faith to rest on. I think the cheeses I salted and put to press that day were as well done as ever. I knew what I had to do; yet it was not merely the grind of a machine. It demanded judgment, accuracy, attention; and it saved me from myself.

The next day I rode down to the post-office. Mr. Harding left me sitting in the wagon in a little pine-wood a few rods from the village shop where the office was kept, while he went for the news, however it might come. It was a hot, quiet autumn day. As yet no leaves were turned, but the indescribable foreboding of death and decay, that breathes in every air and sound of fall, hushed the whole land with funereal quiet; purple asters starred the edges of the road, golden-rods held their feathered masses upright in the paler sunshine, crowds of life everlasting crouched with their dead, yet deathless, blooms on every barren knoll,—a strange, dried sweetness filled the air everywhere. But here, under the pine-trees, the last fires of summer fused from the acute leaves and rough boughs their antique odor of fragrant resins, that has a breath beyond spice, and a perfume surpassing flowers. Both preservative and revivifying, it assailed other avenues of my nature than the sense it at once stimulated and satisfied; for the brain that it entered, through the subtlest of all entrances, expanded with insatiable longings, and fled away from the weary weight of space and sense into some upper air, where the ample ether was keen life and the light immortal knowledge; through all toned to finite capacities by the low whisper of awful, yet sweet, sorrow, that crept from the boughs with that exhaling odor, and breathed to the ear its ocean song of plaintive despair, the very pulse-tune of life and its immutable dead-march toward eternity. In that atmosphere that lulls my brain and exalts it beyond any other known influence I drew deep draughts of rest, and when I heard a man's tread coming, heavy and blundering, along the soft sand foot-path, though I knew by the very weight and stumble of that firm foot that he was blind with grief, I wore a calm face to meet Mr. Harding's blurred eyes, and held out a strong hand to help him find his way to the seat beside me. He thrust a telegram slip into my hands, seized the reins, struck the patient horse he never struck before a blow that sent it off at full speed, and I opened the crumpled slip. Its peculiar ominous mixture of print and writing ran thus:—

> A. Harding, Stoneboro.—Capt. A. H. Banks killed on the field. Private J. Harding missing.—A.J. Bolles, 2d Lieutenant.

"Missing! only missing!" There must have been a great deal of latent hope in my nature to have seized on that frail straw as if it were a rock of refuge; but I did. Cousin Aristarchus looked around at me with eyes of such wonder and grief at my exclamation that I was half vexed.

"Why cousin!" said I,—"*missing* is nothing. He is safe somewhere. We shall hear from him tomorrow."

"Shall we?" said he, vacantly.

"Why, of course we shall! Only think—not dead, like poor Banks; not wounded; only *missing!*"

He whipped the horse again with a fierce stroke, but said nothing. In ten minutes we were at home, and I had told granny. She looked at me with her bright, yet inexpressive, eyes, and said, slowly, "The letter killeth, but the spirit giveth life." What on earth had this to do with me or my news? I was used to her odd speeches, but this one seemed more irrelevant than usual. It haunted me all day in my thoughts of Joe,—merciful thoughts, sent, I believe truly, from above, that I might not be smitten at once, but rather led gently through the valley of the shadow. "The letter killeth!" At last it dawned on me: granny and his father had indeed taken the letter of the message, and their hope was dead. They were old and broken; but I was beginning life, and its vital spirit of love and action upheld me; but, then why should they despair? I did not know then that granny's father, the hero of the race, who died in the Revolution, had been just so reported— "Missing," and found, after bitter weeks of winter, through which wife and babies waited and watched in vain, a stark and stiffened corpse near Ticonderoga, scalped, and pierced with English bullets through heart and limb. No wonder that they despaired.

Slowly the days went on. Cousin Aristarchus more than once resolved to go on and search for Joe; twice was all but ready, and then decided that it was worse than useless, for he could not follow him on the rebel track, and as yet there came no trace of him by report or message. He seemed all bowed and warped by sorrow in mind as well as body; his energy was gone, his life faded out. Oh, how I wished then to be a man! I longed and pined to go and look for Joe. I thought I could have tracked his flight, and rescued him whatever obstacles interposed. So the days crept on into weeks, and heavy gloom settled down upon us, broken only by rare gleams of hope as bits of detail, creeping out in the papers, recounted the death, or the illness, or the wounded condition of one after another at first, like ours, reported missing; gleams that only made the gloom heavier in its return, as the vivid track of lightning serves but to show, in a midnight storm, the awful height and blackness of overhanging clouds full of threat and terror.

By a month's end the blow came. As I said, Captain Banks, son of a near neighbor of ours, had been telegraphed as "killed on the field" by the same message that declared Joe "missing." Fortunately his mother, who was a widow, had left town for a day or two, and did not get the message till another followed close upon it to contradict the first. He had not been killed, but so fearfully wounded, that, seeing his lifeless face and streaming blood, in the panic of defeat he had been left by his men where he lay, with his rebel opponent dead beside him, and the cold corpse-face against his was his first sensation when he recovered from his swoon, somewhere in the dead of night. Happily for him he was found early in the morning alive, but too weak to speak. They took him to a hospital, where he was recognized, and did whatever they could for him; but fever set in, and when he was raving and apparently dying they sent for his mother. Under her care he began at length to recover, and six weeks after the battle, having regained his memory and strength enough to talk, he asked her to write and tell Uncle Harding that he saw Joe shot in the front rank, just before he himself fell. Not only that he saw him shot, but saw him reel to the ground just as a squadron of rebel cavalry charged and swept over him; so there could be no doubt of his fate.

Now, indeed, it was all over,—life and love and hope,—over forever! Like the mad whirl of chaos heaving before God clave it with his divine order, all my soul whirled and staggered. I could not bear it; I *could* not! Like a blind man fighting with a mortal enemy I fought with Fate, for I could not call it Providence then. I could not endure; duty was a blank negation to me. If I could have sunk on the floor and stayed there, unmoving and desperate till death released me, I would have done so; but instincts and habits tormented me forever back into life. Out of that desolate region to which I had fled, that arid desert on whose sands I fell, mad and blind, I was perpetually recalled by little daily needs, by the sting of hunger and the dry lips of thirst; by the demands upon my care and forbearance that others, perhaps suffering as much as I, though I would not believe it, daily made upon me. I have thought since what a mercy it was that He who made us, foreknowing the anguish and the lessons of life, put our souls into the conservating power of bodies. With no lesser wants, no failing of the flesh to distract the spirit from its awful pangs, how mortal would those pangs be! How beyond endurance, how lurid with the horrors of incredible, unimaginable essence and space! No; thank God that we are lower than the angels; for we sin and suffer as no angel could and live.

Mr. Harding was utterly broken down. He sat, with his head upon his hands, in the chimney-corner, hour after hour; nothing moved him. The farm-work he left entirely to his hired man,—a trustworthy person enough, but wanting in judgment and self-reliance. Another of the continual pin-pricks that daily roused me for a moment was his incessant demand for advice and direction. But at length Joe's last words to me recurred to my mind with strange force. What was I doing for him, for his? I saw suddenly what selfish sorrow mine had been; how everything I ought to do had gone undone, as, driven by the restless fury of my grief, I had spent those bright autumn days wandering over hill and field, through lonely woods and across wild ravines, where I startled the partridge and drove the rabbit from his lair; as I tore through bush and brier, regardless of all but the fierce impulse of motion, the necessity of some unreasoning activity; only coming home at the habitual hours of meals and rest, leaving those two other lonely souls to fight their trouble as they best might. I was ashamed now. I am ashamed still to reflect how little healing or constraining influence my religion—such as it was—had upon me. I had not yet been long enough under its influence to have acquired the habit of faith and submission; and under this deadly blow I knew nothing, felt nothing Christian or acquiescent, except the ever-present conviction that even in this whirling storm God was somewhere,— not with me, nor for me; but still living, and unchanged, and just, though all his world slipped away from under my feet like the sliding earth of a nightmare dream. I did not believe he was other than good, but I struck up against Heaven with my bleeding hands, and asked, with horrors of reproach and unbelief, "Why hast thou done this?" nor did Heaven reply!

Just as I have seen a mother with a wayward child, in its first passion of temper and grief, neither punish nor argue with it, but only divert its thoughts with some new story or external object, and then, when the sobs ceased, and the eyes were clear, and calmness had smoothed its fair little face into natural lines, quietly reprove, remonstrate, or even punish; so, as I have since seen, did a diviner love than any mother's guide me, even by means of the very passionate human love that made me rebel, into a calmer sphere. Did he punish thereafter, or break my heart again with love instead of wrath?

I ceased after this to isolate myself, and resumed as best I could my neglected work; but something was necessary to rouse Mr. Harding: what could I do? As I was at work one day in the shed, Lemuel, the hired man, came in over the sill, and, leaning his back against the door, began one of his usual appeals:—

"I declare for't Ann, I don't know what I be agoin' to do with the corn-stalks. Can't you jest step around and give me an idee?"

"I'll ask cousin," said I. Lem. stared, but kept his position, and began to tie a snapper which he produced from his pocket to the end of the long whip he held in his hand. I was glad he stayed behind. So I went into the great kitchen, where a fire of good hickory sticks sparkled and flamed on the hearth, for it was a chill November day. Granny sat in her own place, Mr. Harding on the other side, his head held in both his hands, the gray light from the window striking across its silver mass of tangled curls, and the red firelight flickering on the great, rough hands that concealed both face and forehead. I went up to him and stooped down beside his chair.

"Father," said I.

He started as if a shot pierced him; his hands dropped, and his dim, bloodshot eyes looked up with wild inquiry. I put one hand on his knee and laid my head on it; that was an old childish trick of Joe's I had often heard of, as being the only caress his father ever endured from either of his children. He was neither a gentle nor a demonstrative man.

"Father," said I again, "Lemuel wants to know where he shall put the corn-stalks."

Mr. Harding did not speak at once. He gave a low groan, like a sigh; then—"Lord, forgive me! I am worse'n a dumb ox. You come with me, my child."

He got up from his chair and shook himself, like a person bent on throwing off sleep, reached his old hat from the nail, and my shawl and hood, which hung beside it. As we went out of the door granny said audibly, "A Father to the fatherless, and the widow's God." He held my hand with a tighter grasp as the words met his ear, and held it still while we went the rounds of the barn, and he gave his directions to Lem. as clear and well-judged as ever, every now and then turning to me for an opinion. I knew afterward that Joe had said to his father nearly what he had said to me, and asked him, moreover, to care for and comfort me, if care and comfort should ever be needed as they were now. From this day he always called me "My child" and I always said "Father" to him.

So we settled down into the dull, gray calm of life again; very silent, very quiet, we all were. Granny now and then volunteered a proverb or a text, as strangely fit to the mood, rather than any occasion, as her utterances usually were. I remember once when Mr. Harding had gone to the village, and I sat by his empty chair sewing, I unconsciously drew a long, sobbing sigh. Granny took out her needle from the sheath, and laid her stocking down, saying, as she did so in a dreamy way, "Yet doth he devise means that his banished be not expelled from him." What did she mean? The words fell softly on my tried soul, yet there was neither special promise nor hope in them for my peculiar want; yet they sung in my thoughts long after, as if persisting on some tender errand, mysterious still to me.

Soon it was time to make Thanksgiving preparations. Last year how different had this all been! What dreadful changes had passed over us since! Cousin Martha and Joe both gone,—what had we to be thankful for? I had paused before going downstairs one morning, when these bitter thoughts had roused me long before light, to look out at the east from my window. A low range of hills barricaded the valley some two or three miles from our house; and now, lying level on their tops, were long bars of amber, flushing at the edges with red, that told of a sunrise far away, but sure incoming, while through the gray sky above that pallid blue streak on the horizon a dying aurora pulsated in flashes of faint light, that fled and throbbed out again, and fled once more, and quivered anew with mystic splendor that thrilled me to see. Strange and fair it was, that cold, bright meeting of dawn and the northern night-lightning; and strangely portentous, too, it seemed to me. Was that a "sign in the sky?"—were these fatal wars foreboding the world's great peace?—was it good or evil that danced and flickered in those ice-glittering flashes above?

Thanksgiving day came at last. My sole pleasure in its preparations had been in carrying out my resolve that no poor soul I knew of, within our township, should go without a good dinner to-day. Somebody should be thankful if I was not. So I had sent Lemuel round with a big basket of pies, and chickens, and tongues, and other necessities of Thanksgiving, the day before; and now, having laid out my dinner on the side-table in the summer parlor, as far as its cold viands were concerned, and leaving the girl to look after granny, who seemed feebler than usual of late, and giving her strong charges about the turkey, and the potatoes, and the turnips, that already were in their respective corners hissing, and bubbling, and sending savory odors up the chimney, I dressed myself in my best, and set off for church with "father."

Our old minister had gone away to keep Thanksgiving with his son in Boston, and to-day a stranger was to preach for us. Our village choir was a good one for the country, with several fine, though untrained, voices, and one remarkable soprano, that seemed in its purity and accuracy to defy the need of instruction; and as it rose alone in the anthem before service, and wandered along the exquisite music of those words, "Rest in the Lord; oh, rest in the Lord! Wait patiently for him, and he shall give thee thy heart's desire," more than one dull eye glittered with tears that did not fall. But on my heart tears lay like lead, nor sprung to cool my hot eyes. Ah! what patient waiting could ever bring to me my heart's desire? Not God himself, I said, could restore this ruined past!

I looked across the aisle and saw Mrs. Banks, the captain's mother; her handkerchief was at her face, but she wept for joy,—her son was home again, weak and helpless, but at home! It was Thanksgiving to her; but for me there was no restoration. Sitting there quiet in the corner of the pew, unable to exert myself to dispel the bitter thoughts crowding upon me, I became their prey. Hymn and prayer passed by unheeded. I neither heard the text nor the sermon till, when it was about half over, suddenly these words roused me:—

"But there is still heaven to be thankful for. Whatever sorrows bereave us here, whatever fatal mistakes darken our lives, whatever irredeemable losses befall us, we may yet rest in the Lord, and wait patiently for him in the little life that remains; for beyond this world's gain or loss, high in the serene air of heaven, when existence ceases to be a lesson and becomes vivid life, there and only there shall he give us our heart's desire in its immortal fullness. Here knowledge is defiled, love is imperfect, purity the result of fiery trial, wealth rusted with covetousness; but in heaven is the very native country of pure knowledge, perfect love, utter sinlessness, and riches that neither moth nor rust corrupt, that bless and curse not."

He went on to enumerate what we had to be thankful for, even under the reign of anarchy and war; but on these few sentences that I have written I dwelt till peace brooded over my tired heart. Yes! there was heaven to come; and an object still left to life,—to grow into fitness for that rest and its reuniting.

After church we went home without staying to speak to the neighbors, who seemed to understand and respect our silence. They all went home with groups of children and grandchildren about them; we were alone.

Soon as possible I had dinner on the table. I wanted to have it through; I wanted the day done. Anniversaries are like old wounds that reopen and bleed every year. I hurried to have the observances of this one over with. So we sat down to dinner—three, where last year had been five! Cousin Martha's fair, wan face, with its scarlet flush on cheek and lip, smiling beside granny; Joe's manly, sunburnt visage and handsome figure on the other.

We sat down in perfect silence. Mr. Harding carved, and we all went through at least the form of eating. Still in that dead silence, when just as I was about to lay down my knife and fork, a wagon came rapidly down the road and stopped at our door. "Lemuel come back from the post-office," said father.

But was that halting step in the entry Lemuel's?

The door flung open, and there stood Joe. Sorrow is easy to describe, but what words can tell the incredible thrill of such joy as this? For the first time in my life I lost all consciousness for a blind blank moment. I did not faint,—for I never faint,—but I knew nothing from the moment I saw the door open on him till I found both his arms round me and my head lying against him as I still sat in my chair. It's no use trying to tell it. A few, blessed as I, have snatched this blossom out of blood-red battle-fields; they will know.

It seems Joe had fallen, as Captain Banks said, from two musket-bullets that pierced at once the upper part of his left arm; fortunately for him they were not Minié-bullets, but the old kind. Then the cavalry charge swept over him, and a horse stepping on his right leg broke it badly; he escaped marvelously with his life, and fortunately no artery was ruptured; but he lay on the field three days and three nights, was then picked up by a farmer,—a Virginian and a Union man,—who, passing by the field, heard him groan; he picked him up, took him home, drove off to the nearest doctor to be found, and had his leg set, and his wounds dressed; but Joe was too weak to talk or think, and before he had strength to do either, fever set in, with delirium, and in consequence they neither knew who he was or where he came from. But the woman of the house nursed him like a mother. She had two sons fighting in the West with Rosecrans, and she said it was for thinking of them that she never let a soldier pass her door hungry or thirsty, and took such care of Joe. If gratitude and blessing and prayers can keep that woman's sons alive and well, they will come back to her scatheless!

So for two months he lay there between life and death. Then he wrote, but the letter was lost, or delayed, or missent; and through his slow convalescence he expected to see his father or me daily, and so wrote no more till, as soon as he could sit up long enough, he got to Hagerstown, and from there home. True, his leg had been badly set, and he never would walk without limping, and his arm still lay in a sling; but it was Joe! No matter how battered or broken, no matter how wan and thin, he was back again!

The next week I laid aside my heavy crape and bombazine for a white dress, and we were married. Still bent and grave, but with a bright smile, father put both his arms round me and kissed me for the first time in his life. "My *dear* child!" was all he said.

And the week after I put on those mourning garments again, for granny was gone. The only words she had spoken since Joe came home, except in answer to some question, were: "He that saveth his life shall lose it, but he that loseth his life shall find it." She sank into a sort of lethargy, and fell asleep like a contented child.

It is winter now. Heavy snow falls as I write, drifting from the north-east, and settling, shroud-like, over the earth; but in the house, at home, there is no climate but summer.

God has given me my heart's desire.

Margaret Bronson

Elizabeth Stuart Phelps Ward

Iknow you are tired enough of tales of war, and that your own dark memories of the sealed record of the nation's bloody baptism need no fresh reminders. My story does not concern a battle, but a woman; and how can I help it if she lived down there on the border, so surrounded and hemmed in by conflict and combatants, by scenes of peril and blood and death, that they must necessarily interweave themselves with the controlling events of her life? I hardly know what you would have thought of her if you had seen her standing there alone on the lawn in the haze of that sultry June evening. You would have stopped involuntarily, as before some striking picture. A woman with a certain regal bearing in the drooping of her shoulders, in the position of her hands, in the curve of her neck, in the very folds of her lustreless black silk dress and the mantle of white crape that fell over it—a graceful woman certainly; a well-poised head held a little loftily, perhaps; a face somewhat pale contrasted with the hair that was pushed back from it, and features regular as a statue's.—A beautiful woman then? That would depend partly on yourself, partly on her mood. A particular curl in the bright color of her lips, an arch of her eyebrow, a sharp, decided tone about the whole contour of her face, might at any time and always have repelled you. Or, if you had seen her smile as she could smile if she chose, as she did not often you might wish Murillo could have painted her. The slant sunbeams were flecking the grass and the trees above her, touching spots of gold, too, upon her dark dress. You would have noticed rather her independence of their effect than that they added any thing by it; the play of light and shade and color did not seem necessary to her as to many women. You would fancy that she might stand in the dimness of a dungeon unchanged. In this circumstance—as often through lesser avenues the soul finds voice—lay the key to Miss Bronson's nature.

People were rather dubious on the subject of a young woman who carried pistols, had no desire to marry, and was not afraid of guerrillas. It was outré, it evinced discontent with her sphere; it was—it really was— "strong-minded." Very likely. And you don't like the word? I am sorry, for it seems to be appropriate, and I am obliged to use it. It and she fitted well into the life she had led. For a mother, she had only the memory of a kiss on a dead face; for childhood and girlhood, a long, luxurious dream with her own fancies, and the sole companionship of that uncompanionable, silent father, who, dying six months ago, left her as inheritance enough of his own Northern temperament to cool the heats of her Southern blood; a well-ordered plantation, and a crowd of model slaves moulded after the most sacred pattern of the "institution"—perhaps because their master was too much of a gentleman to be grossly cruel—perhaps because he found occasion to pacify within himself certain clamorous memories of the faith of his fathers.

As to the slaves, Miss Bronson freed them within a month after the old man gave her his last kiss; she would have done it the day after his funeral, except out of respect for him. This utterly illogical and inconsequent act was doubtless the foundation of the objectionable epithet aforesaid, which horrified rumor had attached to her. As for the plantation, she carried its business on by herself, with such of the negroes who chose to remain with her as she could support; smiled when the neighbors were scandalized that Miss Bronson should reduce herself to such disgraceful poverty; chose neither relative, friend, nor husband for company, but passed her days in solitude and the gloom of the old rooms which had such a foreign hush in them, from missing the dead man's silence. She might have been lonely, for she loved him; or she might not. No one knew but herself.

The haze had blotted out the golden flecks on her dress and hair, and the twilight had fallen heavily, while she stood there watching the west. She began at last to pace back and forth under the trees, in a peculiar, nervous way she had, which was more like that of a man than of a woman, yet not unwomanly nor ungraceful.

A footstep in the street, and a voice at the grate calling her name, aroused her from her reverie. She turned her head slowly, and stopped her walk.

"Mr. M'Ginley, I think? It is rather dark."

"Yes, Miss Bronson."

She did not advance to meet him or invite him to enter, but stood as she had stood, watching the sunset, in that statue-like attitude which could not be any thing but haughty, if she tried to make it so. Yet I doubt if she knew it. The young man hesitated an instant, then came in, and up the graveled walk.

"Am I intruding?"

"Intruding? Oh no."

"I should be sorry if I were, because—"

"Are you alone?"

It was not Miss Bronson's custom to interrupt; she was too well-bred; he knew that.

"Yes," he said.

"It is not safe, I suppose?" she questioned, busied with drawing the crape over her shoulders.

"Perhaps not; that is a matter of very little consequence, however."

The shade of bitterness in his tone could not have escaped her, but she took no notice of it; she occupied herself in picking a blossom of the scarlet trumpet-flower that trailed over the trees, then threw it away.

"Won't you sit down? You may be tired with your walk."

He thanked her, and refused with some reserve, placing the garden-chair for her. She preferred to stand.

"You do not wear the gray, I see, when you take your strolls," she said, glancing at the eagles on his sleeve. They had been bright once, but were dull with long service now.

"Hardly—not even in *this* hospitable town. I prefer, under all circumstances, to carry the face as well as the heart of loyalty. If I recollect rightly, I believe I have never been afraid or ashamed of this uniform."

The rough private's dress formed a strong contrast to the elegance of her's but it was more than balanced by something in his deep-set eyes, and a certain pressure of his thin lips; perhaps a word of Mrs. Browning's—*masterful*—would have expressed it. Some such thought as this may have crossed her mind, for she glanced from the uniform up into his weather-stained face. Then she looked away. She may have remembered just then the home he had left, the friends he had estranged, the hardships and perils he had borne and braved, for this humble place among his country's workers. Miss Bronson had many theories of her own concerning sham patriotism, but she knew the ring of the real coin when she heard it. It was another evidence of the justice of that unfashionable epithet I have alluded to that she had been loyal from the fall of Sumter, and that she had had the courage to say so when occasion offered.

"On the contrary"—with some brightness in her eyes— "you should be proud of it."

She was kind to think so, he said, and said it wondering if there were a servant on her plantation to whom she might not have spoken the same words as graciously.

"It has been rough work in its day, Miss Bronson, but we are rather still in camp just now. Are you not *very* lonely some of these summer evenings?"

The abruptness of the question, asked with the look and tone with which he asked it, would have embarrassed many women. To Miss Bronson, question, tone, and look alike seemed to be not more than any other idle chat. Except for the chill in her voice, when she said, raising her eyelids in her slow, haughty way:

"Lonely? Why should I be?"

M'Ginley bit his lip.

"Are not my grounds looking well, Mr. M'Ginley?" turning, with a polite, careless smile, which on her face was a mere glitter. "The guerrillas have let me alone so far, except that little patch of cotton down in the south field, which was of small consequence."

"I wish they had not touched the south field, Miss Bronson."

"Why that particularly? it could easily be spared."

"Because I have pleasant associations with it."

She remembered too—he knew she did—the days when they had played there as children, at mimic house-keeping on the mimic plantation—the long, long sunny days bright with pictures of blossoms and birds and cloudless skies, and the little dark-eyed girl who used to go out among them with him, hand in hand. She *must* remember. Yet if she did she gave no sign. The incredulous arch of her eyebrow, which was her only answer, seemed to sting the young man. He turned quickly, some sudden flush mounting to his forehead, stopped in his slow walk down the path and faced her.

"Miss Bronson, look at me, if you please."

She complied, because she chose to; she made it very evident that was her only reason. His face just then had a look Miss Bronson was little used to meeting, much less to enduring quietly.

"You *do* remember."

She smiled.

"Playing with you in the south field? Oh, yes; I have a good memory."

"You do *not* remember it unpleasantly?"

"Mr. M'Ginley, it is somewhat chilly standing still so long." He turned sharply away from her and strode down to the gate. She continued her walk as indifferently as if nothing had happened to interrupt her.

"Are you going? Well, I wish you a pleasant evening and a safe walk."

He smiled bitterly.

"A man's life is the most worthless investment he has, in these times. If the little dividends should stop before I see you again—"

He waited, apparently for some expression of interest from her. But there was not a word or a look. She stood perfectly still, with her eyes on the darkening road.

"In that case I thought I should like to tell you why I left camp to-night. Do you wish to know?"

"Oh, I'll leave that to you; if you chose to tell me, you may."

Again that look which Miss Bronson was not used to enduring . His eyes were on fire; the compression of his lips seemed absolute pain—perhaps she did not see it.

"I *do* choose to tell you. I came to see you; if I had seen you for a moment unknown to yourself, my object would have been gained. I had not expected the honor of a conversation with you. I am obliged to you for your condescension."

He waited, before he bade her good-evening, to watch her a moment; with that look which on a man's face shows the crisis of some great agony in the soul—a look which the accident of his death might well stamp on Miss Bronson's memory as long as she could remember anything. But she had not a word for him—not one. She stood there in her elegant calm, so near to him that she could hear his sharp, hard breathing, as far from him as if oceans rolled between them. He remembered afterward that her silence was unusual even for her; also a certain strained repose in the folding of her hands which caught his eye, but which, in the passion of the moment, served only to work into a wandering fancy of his, that he was trying to move a block of beautiful marble.

Miss Bronson stood just where he had left her, long after he had gone. Once she started, with a quick motion, as if she would have called him back; then stopped herself, with a little scorn in her smile.

She knew this man loved her—loved her even to the peril of his life. Well, what then? You would have wondered, if you had seen her break sharply into her quick pacing on the graveled walk again; if you had watched her knotted forehead and cold, set lips, you would have wondered whether Robert M'Ginley, who saw in her a very different woman from that solitary, self-sufficient figure, was dreaming of a shadow, or if he understood Mrs. Bronson better than she did herself. Back and forth, forth and back she went on her nervous walk, some excitement in her face serving only to give it a deeper chill. Was M'Ginley a fool to want such a woman at his fireside? You, perhaps, would have said so, if you had seen her then, and have turned away as you would turn from an iceberg. Some one very candidly told him the same thing upon one occasion—a man who prided himself on his translation of women's faces.

"Why, M'Ginley, you haven't but one eye open. She's a beautiful woman, but she'd turn a fellow's home into Pandemonium. It would be a violation of nature for her to be a wife. *She* must be the man, and she'd rule every thing with a rod of iron. To yield one inch of her own will would be torture to her."

"I do not think so," repled M'Ginley, with a quiet smile. He might still have retained his opinion, for he was not a man who formed or rejected beliefs lightly; but he would not have smiled if he had seen her once that evening stop there in the darkening shadows and clench her delicate hands upon her breast with a passion that fitted the half-frightened defiance in her eyes. Defiance? Of whom? Of what? Perhaps of herself.

You think I am telling you of a woman who belongs only in poetry and romance. I assure you that I am not.

It was about an hour after M'Ginley had left her that one of the servants came hurriedly to the parlor window, near which she was sitting alone in the dark.

"Miss Margaret!"

"Oh, is it you, Dan? You gave Prince the extra quart of meal, as I told you, and sent my message to the gardener?"

"Yes, Miss Margaret, de work's all done gone out ob de way for de night. 'Tain't dat ar I come fur. 'Pears like I knows someting you'd oughter be telled on."

Something in the negro's face arrested her attention.

"You may come in, Dan. What is it?"

"Nobody hedn't oughter to be hearin' ob it, Miss Margaret. Der's no tellin' what might become ob we all ef dey did."

"You may close the window, Dan."

He closed it, and the door. He said then a few words to her scarcely above a whisper.

She changed color—as much as she ever did.

"Are you sure?"

"Yes, clar sure, Miss Margaret. I war huntin' fur sassafras fur my ole woman—she's sot her heart on't she's done got de kersumption, an' der warn't nothin' for't but de sassafras—an' dey come 'long atween de trees— two ob 'em—an' I heered every word, an' I neber breaf till dey get by, an' dey don' see me. Ef dey'd see me—laws! Miss Margaret, I wouldn't a'ben here ter tell."

"What was the time to be, Dan?"

"Jes' ten 'clock, case I heerd 'em name it over affer dey's got trough."

Miss Bronson looked her watch.

"You may lock up well, Dan, and the people can come into the kitchen if they are at all frightened. There is, however, nothing, I think to fear. They will have work enough without coming into the town. And, Dan, I do not care to be disturbed this evening. I wish to be alone. Tell Rose and Eliza, if any thing is wanted, to wait till I call them."

"Yes, Miss Margaret."

She took off her crape mantle and began to fold it up, while she listened to his retreating footsteps; she smoothed every crease and carefully straightened the fringe. There was something curious in the mechanical action; perhaps an intensity of excitement which a word or a cry would have weakened.

Then she went to her own room, divested her dress of some of its feminine encumbrances, threw over her shoulders a dark, hooded cloak, examined her revolver and loaded it. After that she went hurriedly down stairs, out of the door, and into the street.

A great lurid moon glared through the mist that night, and the clouds that the wind tossed by it were stained with sullen red. M'Ginley watched it rise over the hill where they were encamped, with some odd fancy about its color and the last long day when it should set forever. His face had paled within the last hour. A certain hungry longing had crept into it—that longing which can not be mistaken, and which is so pitiful to see, especially in a man, and a man like Robert M'Ginley. I do not mean that he would have sought or deliberately chosen death; he was too thoroughly soldierly in the warp and woof of his nature for that. Margaret Bronson could never make a sentimentalist, or that most cowardly of cowards—a suicide—out of him. But simply that, standing there apart from his comrades and their cheerful camp-fire talk that night, with the smothered passion of the reddened moonlight above and around him, and the memory of that one woman's face for his sole companionship, he may have thought—Well, I fancy death seemed a pleasant thing and fair to look upon. It had become so familiar to him in the life he led; it so dogged his steps and hedged him in; it talked with him in his dreams, and woke with him in the cool summer dawns; it basked in the glare of the sunlight and lurked in the evening shadows; it and his troubled life hung forever beside him, balanced in the chance of a single shot. He may have wondered, as he stood there with his face turned toward the sullen moon, and the group of pines below it, beyond which her home was hidden—he may have wondered a little—we all like to speculate at times as to what the world will be when we go out of it—whether the sight of his life-blood would thaw one jot of Miss Bronson's frozen elegance. Probably its contrast to the dazzling white of her own folded hands would not be pleasant. Probably she would beg them to care for him decently, and bury him out of her sight. Possibly she would say the country was making a terrible sacrifice of its young men— then go and dress for dinner.

Looking down through the trees where the shades of the valley hung and deepened, his eye caught at last the outline of a dim form threading its way through them. Its motion was rapid, its path direct to the camp. As it came out into the light in a little opening among the oaks, he saw the flutter of a woman's dress. He watched it curiously as it began the slow ascent over fallen trees and stumps and tangled underbrush. It was a dark, hooded figure, somewhat tall and erect, with a certain fearless disregard of the obstacles in the path, which was more natural to a man than a woman, and gave him for the instant a suspicion of disguise and treachery. Just then, however, the light struck full on a hand raised to push aside a dead bough—a slender, jeweled hand, that had an indescribable air of familiarity to him in the strained repose of its fingers. He saw also with distinctness her black dress whose trailing folds had been shortened out of reach of briers and rocks. She came up the slope under a shadow, through a gleam of lurid mist, then out upon a projecting rock beside him, where she stood quite still. Her hood had fallen off, her face was full in the light of the camp-fire.

"Miss Bronson!"

"I believe so."

"*You* here, and alone!"

"I here and alone, Mr. M'Ginley, owing to the little circumstance that I have discovered a plot to surprise your camp to-night, with a force very conveniently outnumbering yours, every man of them thoroughly educated blood-hounds. Their calculations, if I remember rightly, comprised the butchery of two-thirds of you at the very lowest estimate; they attack you on the cast side, at your weak point by the ravine. As to time," she coolly took out her watch, "if they had the virtue of punctuality they would have been here five minutes ago."

"You are sure of this?"

"Perfectly, one of my people heard the whole thing discussed in the woods below you there. You remember Dan, perhaps? He is of a somewhat excitable temperament, but as to creating a story of any magnitude, it would be altogether too much of a tax upon his intellect. I think you may expect your visitors at any moment."

All the soldier flashed into his face; for the moment he forgot her.

"Colonel, boys, where's the Colonel?"

She watched him as he sprang away from her. If he had seen her face he would have known how much he had heightened her respect for him because he did forget her on such an errand.

It was only for a moment. He was back beside her then; his face was pale.

"Margaret, it is terrible, you have saved us, but *you*—"

"I shall do very well. Why not?"

"You don't know what a hell you have come into—*you!*" he passed his hand over his forehead; the great drops stood on it. "My God! If I could get you safe at home—only get you home!"

She smiled.

"I am not afraid. I should hardly have undertaken this little expedition if I had been afraid." A sudden confusion prevented his reply—the sound of the Colonel's voice, quick orders, and the men falling into line. Miss Bronson tossed off her cloak and took her pistol from her belt.

"What are you going to do?"

"Fight."

"Miss Bronson!"

She threw off his hand from hers.

"Why not? I will not hide here in the bushes and die like a coward; no, not even for a look like that, Mr. M'Ginley. You know I could not go back if I would. See, they are calling you."

The quick orders grew impatient; the ranks swept by them. M'Ginley fell into his place at the end of the line. Miss Bronson stepped beside him. He said but one word after that, "Margaret!"

Her fingers stirred a little on the pistol; her glittering smile played all over her face. He knew then that she would have despised him if he had argued the case by so much as another syllable.

"They are coming," she said, with a bit of triumph in her smile.

Her face was worth seeing, when the sergeant discovered her, and quietly ordered her out of the ranks.

"If you can tell me any reason, Sir, why I should *not* fight, I should like to know it."

"Agin orders, mum."

"But you are short of men."

"Beggin' your pardon, mum, I believe you hain't a man."

"What does that matter? I have no more fancy for looking on idle."

"Can't help it, mum, sorry to disappoint a lady; but there's my orders. Wounded and women-folks and young uns to the rear. So, if you please mum, you'd better fall out."

Miss Bronson obeyed in a silent disgust. A woman's will *versus* military discipline. Certainly it was a hard case.

A rustling of dead leaves in the ravine, a tramping of many feet, a flash of bayonets on the brow of the hill; then a vision of dark, exultant faces, a yell, a cheer, a thunder that woke all the echoes sleeping far down the valley; and the quiet camp became a battle-field.

The deserted fires flashing up broadly, darting rifts of light in through the smoke and horror, showed Miss Bronson standing under the trees. She stood there for five minutes. Then the fair-haired boy, fighting beside M'Ginley, fell with a ball through his heart.

When M'Ginley turned his head he saw her in the vacant place—the dead boy's musket in her hand.

"I prefer to be here," she said.

Probably military discipline would have had a word to say to its late defeated antagonist, if it had not been altogether too busy just then in the confusion of a charge. The picture, bright in the fitful glare, was one long to be remembered—the woman with her colorless, calm face and eyes on fire, the shadow of a smile still lingering on her lips, her black hair fallen low on her shoulder, and the fearless aim of the hand so womanly, so dazzling, so foreign to its deathly work.

She fought like a veteran. M'Ginley, so near to her, knew how her teeth were set, and could see her breast heave with her sharp, hard breathing. Once she looked up into his face.

"I don't know much about it; tell me if I am wrong."

The tone was a tone in which Margaret Bronson was unused to speaking; he heard every cadence of it above the roar of the musketry, and in that hour when she seemed to have thrown off her womanhood, he knew that she was nearer to him than ever in all her life before. After that he guided her.

"Aim higher, Margaret."

"You load in too much of a hurry, Margaret; you gain nothing by it."

"Margaret, you are out of the ranks."

So between his own fierce work—and she obeyed him as implicitly as a child. Throughout the whole he used instinctively the name by which he had called her when they played together in the old south field at home. She accepted it as instinctively. I think she liked it. Possibly it helped her; as to that you could not tell; she never quailed for an instant; her face never lost its colorless calm, her eyes their fire, nor her hand its fearless aim.

The camp-fires were dying low into their ashes; the moon's sullen glare from the treetops showed through the billows of smoke a breach in the enemy's ranks. The lines staggered and broke on the brow of the hill.

"We have them," said M'Ginley, with a grim smile, and fell with the words on his lips.

The ranks closed again and swept on victorious down the slope far into the valley to finish their work. But the beautiful woman's face was not among them.

She knelt down on the ground where he had fallen; his blood stained her dress in pitiful contrast to its silken richness.

"Can you tell me where it is?"

She spoke quietly; if she had had all the knowledge of the surgeons, and every means of saving his life at her command instead of being ignorant and alone in that desolated place, she could not have spoken more quietly; you could not have seen that a nerve trembled.

"It is nothing—only in my arm, I think," he said, feebly; "you can get home now, Margaret—go; don't stop to think of me."

"I *shall* think of you. I intend to save you."

She looked about her for a moment. At the right a rebel lay dead in the bushes. A few yards beyond another—dead or dying, for he stirred a little. No other human being was in sight. The distant camp-fires were out. The moon hung angrily in the mist; far down the valley the noise of the conflict was growing fainter; M'Ginley's hot blood was still staining her dress. Her sense of utter helplessness was written for an instant on her face; but it was turned away from him and he did not see it.

"You must stay here"—she spoke rapidly and decidedly—"you must stay here a little while. I shall help you into the bushes here out of sight, if there are stragglers round. I will bring some one that can take care of you. I think I can stop the flowing of this blood before I go."

He was too weak to remonstrate. She took out her delicate laced handkerchief and tried to smile.

"If I only had one of Eliza's cotton ones! It is so much cobweb."

"Hold on, missis! You mought as well not spile that ere bit of non-sense, and save yerself the trouble ef bloodyin' yer pretty hands. I've got a little business to do up with that Yankee sweet'heart o'yourn."

She sprang up, with her hand on her revolver.

The dying rebel had risen to his feet; there were no signs of death upon him; he had not so much as a wound. That he was a man of iron muscle, with brawny arms bared, and his bayonet dripping with blood, she saw; that his face was the face of a fiend, she felt.

"What's the matter with yer? Struck dumb? Purty good-looking gal ye are, any ways. Shall be sorry to skeer ye, but I'm 'blighed to settle up 'counts with that 'ere chap; and you'd better git out of the way, ef ye ain't partiklar 'bout seein' it did."

She stepped out into the open path. M'Ginley called her back; but she made no answer.

"You shall not touch him: he is a wounded man."

"Hoity, toity, pretty mistress! We'll see about that. He killed my boy in th' fight, he did. Little chap was drafted in las' week. He's lyin' bak thar 'mong the tents. I'll have my pay fur that. Didn't the little fellow lie an' groan? An' I'll see *him* lie an' groan, an' send him whar he b'longs: yer mought jes' as well make up yer mind to't firs' as las'. An' I wouldn't screech ef I was you, 'cause it won't make no odds ter me."

He laughed, wiping his dripping bayonet on his sleeve. I suppose most women would have fallen on their knees at this crisis, have pleaded and sobbed, wrung their hands, and made allusions to his wife or his mother; also to some faint possibility termed his better nature. Margaret Bronson read the brutish instinct of revenge in the man's face too thoroughly for that; she knew it would be but wasted time, and time was precious.

She stepped up to him, with her fingers clasped on her deathly weapon as steadily as they had clasped it all that horrible night.

"Margaret!"

It was M'Ginley's anguished voice. She heard it. The man, wiping his bayonet, looked into her white still face with dull wonder.

"What ye up to? I'm goin' to work now."

"You are not going to touch him."

"That 'ere's purty talk, mistress, when I dropped dead o'purpose for the chance to run him through—very purty talk!"

"Step back there! If you come another step you are a dead man."

"Should be sorry to fight a gal; have done it, though, 'fore now; an' gal or no gal, I'll put an end to the chap. Here, you Yank! It's time to be a sayin' your prayers."

The bayonet gleamed within a yard of Margaret Bronson's heart.

"Either you or I are dead before you stir," she said. The red light struck full on her face.

"Margaret! Margaret!"

She quivered a little, but her eyes did not move from the steel that flashed just then in a moonbeam.

M'Ginley, trying to crawl to his feet, fell, repeating her name over feebly. He could not reach her. She heard him groan. She was very pale, but she stood like a statue.

The man laughed; as men will laugh upon a volcano.

"Come, come, my pretty fire-brand; I reckon we've had enough of this 'ere play."

The bayonet flashed; the face darkened; he threw up his arms, and, with an oath that she heard on still nights for years and years of her life, fell backward down upon the rocks.

The Doctor, coming out of the parlor where they had laid M'Ginley on the couch, found Miss Bronson washing her hands.

"You're not at it again! You were doing that very thing when I came out after the bandages, Miss Bronson."

She laughed—nervously.

"I don't know. Was I? I had forgotten it."

"You are too white, let me feel your pulse. I *should* like to know how you managed to get him down here?"

"I believe I came down after Dan and Caesar, didn't I? Let me think; yes—that was it. I believe I am a little tired."

"A baby would give up the ghost with such a pulse; you must have stimulant. Do you know that you can not stand?"

"Yes, I can; nothing is the matter. I shall do very well."

But she sat down weakly, and leaned her forehead on her hand.

"You don't ask how my patient is, Miss Bronson?"

"I supposed you would not wish to be annoyed with questions in a dangerous case."

"It is not dangerous; it is a severe flesh wound and slight fracture, but with suitable care there's no danger about it. He is quiet now—comfortable, he says. He wishes to see you."

She rose slowly.

"Are you sure?"

"Is it a very impossible supposition when you have saved his life? My dear Miss Bronson, you are somewhat mazed by your night's work, surely. I shall insist upon a glass of brandy."

"No, you are very good; I would rather not. If you are sure he wishes to see me I will go in."

She went in—not as Miss Bronson had ever entered her own parlor before; her step was faltering, perhaps timid.

"Margaret."

She came across the room at his call, and stood beside him with her head bent, her hands folded tightly into each other. The crimson stains on her rich dress, her falling hair which she had neglected or forgotten to arrange, and the flutter of her drooping eyelids, were in sharp contrast to her usual elegant repose. Yet I think she was not the less beautiful. Perhaps to Robert M'Ginley she was not less imperial.

"Margaret," he said, feebly, "I wanted to see you."

She sank down on the floor so low that she could look up into his face, and he saw in her eyes what he had never seen there before—tears.

"Margaret! Why, Margaret!"

A sudden light shone in his pallid face; perhaps it dazzled her; she bent her head.

"Are you *sure* you wanted to see me?"

"Margaret, look at me."

She looked at him.

"I thought"—she trembled in every nerve, this woman who had gone into battle with a smile—"I thought you would not want to see me. I was afraid you would always think of me up there in the blood and smoke, it seems so terrible now it is over. I wonder if I shall ever forget it?"

"You seem to forget that you saved my life," he said huskily.

The words stung her somehow.

"I do not want you to be grateful to me."

She turned away her head—not haughtily, but very humbly; it drooped again so low that her hair fell over her face.

"Margaret."

She stirred a little.

"Margaret, I have loved you a great while, but I never loved you as I did to-night."

The Lamp of Psyche

Edith Wharton

Delia Corbett was too happy; her happiness frightened her. Not on theological grounds, however; she was sure that people had a right to be happy; but she was equally sure that it was a right seldom recognized by destiny. And her happiness almost touched the confines of pain—it bordered on that sharp ecstasy which she had known, through one sleepless night after another, when what had now become a reality had haunted her as an unattainable longing.

Delia Corbett was not in the habit of using what the French call *gros mots* in the rendering of her own emotions; she took herself, as a rule, rather flippantly, with a dash of contemptuous pity. But she felt that she had now entered upon a phase of existence wherein it became her to pay herself an almost reverential regard. Love had set his golden crown upon her forehead, and the awe of the office allotted her subdued her doubting heart. To her had been given the one portion denied to all other women on earth, the immense, the unapproachable privilege of becoming Laurence Corbett's wife.

Here she burst out laughing at the sound of her own thoughts, and rising from her seat walked across the drawing room and looked at herself in the mirror above the mantelpiece. She was past thirty and had never been very pretty; but she knew herself to be capable of loving her husband better and pleasing him longer than any other woman in the world. She was not afraid of rivals; he and she had seen each other's souls.

She turned away, smiling carelessly at her insignificant reflection, and went back to her armchair near the balcony. The room in which she sat was very beautiful; it pleased Corbett to make all his surroundings beautiful. It was the drawing room of his hotel in Paris; and the balcony near which is wife sat overlooked a small bosky garden framed in ivied walls with a mouldering terra-cotta statue in the center of its cup-shaped lawn. They had now been married some two months and, after traveling for several weeks, had both desired to return to Paris; Corbett because he was really happier there than elsewhere, Delia because she passionately longed to enter as a wife the house where she had so often come and gone as a guest. How she used to find herself dreaming in the midst of one of Corbett's delightful dinners (to which she and her husband were continually being summoned) of a day when she might sit at the same table, but facing its master, a day when no carriage should wait to whirl her away from the brightly lit porte-cochere, and when, after the guests had gone, he and she should be left alone in his library and she might sit down beside him and put her hand in his! The high-minded reader may infer from this that I am presenting him, in the person of Delia Corbett, with a heroine whom he would not like his wife to meet; but how many of us could face each other in the calm consciousness of moral rectitude if our inmost desire were not hidden under a convenient garb of lawful observance?

Delia Corbett, as Delia Benson, had been a very good wife to her first husband; some people (Corbett among them) had even thought her laxly tolerant of "poor Benson's" weaknesses. But then she knew her own; and it is admitted that nothing goes so far toward making us blink the foibles of others as the wish to have them extend a like mercy to ourselves. Not that Delia's foibles were of a tangible nature; they belonged to the order which escapes analysis by the coarse process of our social standards.

Perhaps their very immateriality, the consciousness that she could never be brought to book for them before any human tribunal, made her the more restive under their weight; for she was of a nature to prefer buying her happiness to stealing it. But her rising scruples were perpetually being allayed by some fresh indiscretion of Benson's, to which she submitted with an undeviating amiability which flung her into the opposite extreme of wondering if she didn't really influence him to do wrong—if she mightn't help him to do better. All these psychological subtleties exerted, however, no influence over her conduct which, since the day of her marriage, had been a model of delicate circumspection. It was only necessary to look at Benson to see that the most eager reformer could have done little to improve him. In the first place he must have encountered the initial difficulty, most disheartening to reformers, of making his neophyte distinguish between right and wrong. Undoubtedly it was within the measure even of Benson's primitive perceptions to recognize that some actions were permissible and others were not; but his sole means of classifying them was to try both, and then deny having committed those of which his wife disapproved. Delia had once owned a poodle who greatly desired to sleep on a white fur rug which she destined to other uses. She and the poodle disagreed on the subject, and the latter, though submitting to her authority (when reinforced by a whip), could never be made to see the justice of her demand, and consequently (as the rug frequently revealed) never missed an opportunity of evading it when her back was turned. Her husband often reminded her of the poodle, and, not having a whip or its moral equivalent to control him with, she had long since resigned herself to seeing him smudge the whiteness of her early illusions. The worst of it was that her resignation was such a cheap virtue. She had to be perpetually rousing herself to a sense of Benson's enormities; through the ever-lengthening perspective of her indifference they looked as small as the details of a landscape seen through the wrong end of a telescope. Now and then she tried to remind herself that she had married him for love; but she was well aware that the sentiment she had once entertained for him had nothing in common with the state of mind which the words now represent to her; and this naturally diminished the force of the argument. She had married him at nineteen, because he had beautiful blue eyes and always wore a gardenia in his coat; really, as far as she could remember, these considerations had been the determining factors in her choice. Delia as a child (her parents were since dead) had been a much-indulged daughter, with a liberal allowance of pocketmoney, and permission to spend it unquestioned and unadvised. Subsequently, she used sometimes to look, in a critical humor, at the various articles which she had purchased in her teens; futile chains and lockets, valueless china knickknacks, and poor engravings of sentimental pictures. These, as a chastisement to her taste, she religiously preserved; and they often made her think of Benson. No one, she could not but reflect, would have blamed her if, with the acquirement of a fuller discrimination, she had thrown them all out of the window and replaced them by some object of permanent merit; but she was expected not only to keep Benson for life, but to conceal the fact that her taste had long since discarded him.

It could hardly be expected that a woman who reasoned so dispassionately about her mistakes should attempt to deceive herself about her preferences. Corbett personified all those finer amenities of mind and manners which may convert the mere act of being into a beneficent career; to Delia he seemed the most admirable man she had ever met, and she would have thought it disloyal to her best aspirations not to admire him. But she did not attempt to palliate her warmer feeling under the mast of a plausible esteem; she knew that she loved him, and scorned to disavow that also. So well, however, did she keep her secret that Corbett himself never suspected it, until her husband's death freed her from the obligation of concealment. Then, indeed, she gloried in its confession; and after two years of widowhood, and more than two months of marriage, she was still under the spell of that moment of exquisite avowal.

She was reliving it now, as she often did in the rare hours which separated her from her husband; when presently she heard his step on the stairs, and started up with the blush of eighteen. As she walked across the room to meet him she asked herself perversely (she was given to such obliqueness of self-scrutiny) if to a dispassionate eye he would appear as complete, as supremely well-equipped as she beheld him, or if she walked in a cloud of delusion, dense as the god-concealing mist of Homer. But whenever she put this question to herself, Corbett's appearance instantly relegated it to the limbo of solved enigmas; he was so obviously admirable that she wondered that people didn't stop her in the street to attest her good fortune.

As he came forward now, his renewal of satisfaction was so strong in her that she felt an impulse to seize him and assure herself of his reality; he was so perilously like the phantasms of joy which had mocked her dissatisfied past. But his coat sleeve was convincingly tangible; and, pinching it, she felt the muscles beneath.

"What—all alone?" he said, smiling back her welcome.

"No, I wasn't—I was with you!" she exclaimed; then fearing to appear fatuous, added, with a slight shrug. "Don't be alarmed—it won't last."

"That's what frightens me," he answered, gravely.

"Precisely," she laughed, "and I shall take good care not to reassure you!"

They stood face to face for a moment, reading in each other's eyes the completeness of their communion; then he broke the silence by saying, "By the way, I'd forgotten; here's a letter for you."

She took it unregardingly, her eyes still deep in his; but as her glance turned to the envelope she uttered a note of pleasure.

"Oh, how nice—it's from your only rival!"

"Your Aunt Mary?"

She nodded. "I haven't heard from her in a month—and I'm afraid I haven't written to her either. You don't know how many beneficent intentions of mine you divert from their proper channels."

"But your Aunt Mary has had you all your life—I've only had you two months," he objected.

Delia was still contemplating the letter with a smile, "Dear thing!" she murmured. "I wonder when I shall see her?"

"Write and ask her to come and spend the winter with us."

"What—and leave Boston, and her kindergartens, and associated charities, and symphony concerts, and debating clubs: You don't know Aunt Mary."

"No, I don't. It seems so incongruous that you should adore such a bundle of pendantries."

"I forgive that, because you've never seen her. How I wish you could!"

He stood looking down at her with the all-promising smile of the happy lover. "Well, if she won't come to us we'll go to her."

"Laurence—and leave this!"

"It will keep—we'll come back to it. My dear girl, don't beam so; you make me feel as if you hadn't been happy until now."

"No—but it's your thinking of it!"

"I'll do more than think; I'll act; I'll take you to Boston to see your Aunt Mary."

"Oh, Laurence, you'd hate doing it."

"Not doing it together."

She laid her hand for a moment on his. "What a difference that does make in things," she said, as she broke the seal of the letter.

"Well, I'll leave you to commune with Aunt Mary. When you've done, come and find me in the library."

Delia sat down joyfully to the perusal of her letter, but as her eye traveled over the closely-written pages her gratified expression turned to one of growing concern; and presently, thrusting it back into the envelope, she followed her husband to the library. It was a charming room and singularly indicative, to her fancy, of its occupant's character; the expanse of harmonious bindings, the fruity bloom of Renaissance bronzes, and the imprisoned sunlight of two or three old pictures fitly epitomizing the delicate ramifications of her husband's taste. But now her glance lingered less appreciatively than usual on the warm tones and fine lines which formed so expressive a background for Corbett's fastidious figure.

"Aunt Mary has been ill—I'm afraid she's been seriously ill," she announced as he rose to receive her. "She fell in coming downstairs from one of her tenement house inspections, and it brought on water on the knee. She's been laid up ever since—some three or four weeks now. I'm afraid it's rather bad at her age; and I don't know how she will resign herself to keeping quiet."

"I'm very sorry," said Corbett, sympathetically, "but water on the knee isn't dangerous, you know."

"No—but the doctor says she mustn't go out for weeks and weeks; and that will drive her mad. She'll think the universe has come to a standstill."

"She'll find it hasn't," suggested Corbett, with a smile which took the edge from his comment.

"Ah, but such discoveries hurt—especially if one makes them late in life!"

Corbett stood looking affectionately at his wife.

"How long is it," he asked, "since you have seen your Aunt Mary?"

"I think it must be two years. Yes, just two years; you know I went home on business after—" She stopped; they never alluded to her first marriage.

Corbett took her hand. "Well," he declared, glancing rather wistfully at the Paris Bordone above the mantelpiece, "we'll sail next month and pay her a little visit."

II

Corbett was really making an immense concession in going to America at that season; he disliked the prospect at all times, but just as his hotel in Paris had reopened its luxurious arms to him for the winter, the thought of departure was peculiarly distasteful. Delia knew it, and winced under the enormity of the sacrifice which he had imposed upon himself; but he bore the burden so lightly, and so smilingly derided her impulse to magnify the heroism of his conduct, that she gradually yielded to the undisturbed enjoyment of her anticipations. She was really very glad to be returning to Boston as Corbett's wife; her occasional appearances there as Mrs. Benson had been so eminently unsatisfactory to herself and her relatives that she naturally desired to efface them by so triumphal a re-entry. She had passed so great a part of her own life in Europe that she viewed with a secret leniency Corbett's indifference to his native land; but though she did not mind his not caring for his country she was intensely anxious that his country should care for him. He was a New Yorker, and entirely unknown, save by name, to her little circle of friends and relatives in Boston; but she reflected, with tranquil satisfaction, that, if he were cosmopolitan enough for Fifth Avenue, he was also cultured enough for Beacon Street. She was not so confident of his being altruistic enough for Aunt Mary; but Aunt Mary's appreciations covered so wide a range that there seemed small doubt of his coming under the head of one of her manifold enthusiasms.

Altogether Delia's anticipations grew steadily rosier with the approach to Sandy Hook; and to her confident eye the Statue of Liberty, as they passed under it in the red brilliance of a winter sunrise, seemed to look down upon Corbett with her Aunt Mary's most approving smile.

Delia's Aunt Mary—known from the Back Bay to the Sound End as Mrs. Mason Hayne—had been the chief formative influence of her niece's youth. Delia, after the death of her parents, had even spent two years under Mrs. Hayne's roof, in direct contrast with all her apostolic ardors, her inflammatory zeal for righteousness in everything from baking powder to municipal government; and though the girl never felt any inclination to interpret her aunt's influence in action, it was potent in modifying her judgment of herself and others. Her parents had been incurably frivolous, Mrs. Hayne was incurably serious, and Delia, by some unconscious powers of selection, tended to frivolity of conduct, corrected by seriousness of thought. She would have shrunk from the life of unadorned activity, the unsmiling pursuit of Purposes with a capital letter, to which Mrs. Hayne's energies were dedicated; but it lent relief to her enjoyment of the purposeless to measure her own conduct by her aunt's utilitarian standards.

This curious sympathy with aims so at variance with her own ideals would hardly have been possible to Delia had Mrs. Hayne been a narrow enthusiast without visual range beyond the blinders of her own vocation; it was the consciousness that her aunt's perceptions included even such obvious inutility as hers which made her so tolerant of her aunt's usefulness. All this she had tried, on the way across the Atlantic, to put vividly before Corbett; but she was conscious of a vague inability on his part to adjust his conception of Mrs. Hayne to his wife's view of her; and Delia could only count on her aunt's abounding personality to correct the one-sidedness of his impression.

Mrs. Hayne lived in a wide brick house on Mount Vernon Street, which had belonged to her parents and grandparents, and from which she had never thought of moving. Thither, on the evening of their arrival in Boston, the Corbetts were driven from the Providence Station. Mrs. Hayne had written to her niece that Cyrus would meet them with a "hack"; Cyrus was a sable factotum designated in Mrs. Hayne's vocabulary as a "chore man." When the train entered the station he was, in fact, conspicuous on the platform, his smile shining like an open piano, while he proclaimed with abundant gesture the proximity of "de hack," and Delia, descending from the train into his dusky embrace, found herself guiltily wishing that he could have been omitted from the function of their arrival. She could not help wondering what her husband's valet would think of him. The valet was to be lodged at a hotel: Corbett himself had suggested that his presence might disturb the routine of Mrs. Hayne's household, a view in which Delia had eagerly acquiesced. There was, however, no possibility of dissembling Cyrus, and under the valet's depreciatory eye the Corbetts suffered him to precede them to the livery stable landau, with blue shades and a confidentially disposed driver, which awaited them outside the station.

During the drive to Mount Vernon Street Delia was silent; but as they approached her aunt's swell-fronted domicile she said, hurriedly, "You won't like the house."

Corbett laughed. "It's the inmate I've come to see," he commented.

"Oh, I'm not afraid of her," Delia was almost too confidently rejoined.

The parlormaid who admitted them to the hall (a discouraging hall, with a large-patterned oilcloth and buff walls stenciled with a Greek border) informed them that Mrs. Hayne was above; and ascending to the next floor they found her genial figure, supported on crutches, awaiting them at the drawing room door. Mrs. Hayne was a tall, stoutish woman, whose bland expense of feature was accentuated by a pair of gray eyes of such surpassing penetration that Delia often accused her of answering people's thoughts before they had finished thinking them. These eyes, through the closed fold of Delia's embrace, pierced instantly to Corbett, and never had that accomplished gentleman been more conscious of being called upon to present his credentials. But there was no reservation in the uncritical warmth of Mrs. Hayne's welcome, and it was obvious that she was unaffectedly happy in their coming.

She led them into the drawing room, still clinging to Delia, and Corbett, as he followed, understood why his wife had said that he would not like the house. One saw at a glance that Mrs. Hayne had never had time to think of her house or her dress. Both were scrupulously neat, but her gown might have been an unaltered one of her mother's, and her drawing room wore the same appearance of contented archaism. There was a sufficient number of armchairs, the tables (mostly marble-topped) were redeemed from monotony by their freight of books; but it had not occurred to Mrs. Hayne to substitute logs for hard coal in her fireplace, nor to replace by more personal works of art the smoky expanses of canvas "after" Raphael and Murillo which lurched heavily forward from the walls. She had even preserved the knotty antimacassars on her high-backed armchairs, and Corbett, who was growing bald, resignedly reflected that during his stay in Mount Vernon Street he should not be able to indulge in any lounging.

III

Delia held back for three days the question which burned her lip; then, following her husband upstairs after an evening during which Mrs. Hayne had proved herself especially comprehensive (even questioning Corbett upon the tendencies of modern French art), she let escape the imminent "Well?"

"She's charming," Corbett returned, with the fine smile which always seemed like a delicate criticism.

"Really?"

"Really, Delia. Do you think me so narrow that I can't value such a character as your aunt's simply because it's cast in different lines from mine? I once told you that she must be a bundle of pedantries, and you prophesied that my first sight of her would correct that impression. You were right; she's a bundle of extraordinary vitalities. I never saw a woman more thoroughly alive; and that's the great secret of living—to be thoroughly alive."

"I knew it; I knew it!" his wife exclaimed. "Two such people couldn't help liking each other."

"Oh, I should think she might very well help liking me."

"She doesn't, she admires you immensely; but why?"

"Well, I don't precisely fit into any of her ideals, and the worst part of having ideals is that the people who don't fit into them have to be discarded."

"Aunt Mary doesn't discard anybody," Delia interpolated.

"Her heart may not, but I fancy her judgment does."

"But she doesn't exactly fit into any of your ideals, and yet you like her," his wife persisted.

"I haven't any ideals," Corbett lightly responded. *"Je prends mon bien où je le trouve;* and I find a great deal in your Aunt Mary."

Delia did not ask Mrs. Hayne what she thought of her husband; she was sure that, in due time, her aunt would deliver her verdict; it was impossible for her to leave anyone unclassified. Perhaps, too, there was a latent cowardice in Delia's reticence; an unacknowledged dread lest Mrs. Hayne should range Corbett among the intermediate types.

After a day or two of mutual inspection and adjustment the three lives under Mrs. Hayne's roof lapsed into their separate routines. Mrs. Hayne once more set in motion the complicated machinery of her own existence (rendered more intricate by the accident of her lameness), and Corbett and his wife began to dine out and return the visits of their friends. There were, however, some hours which Corbett devoted to the club or to the frequentation of the public libraries, and these Delia gave to her aunt, driving with Mrs. Hayne from one committee meeting to another, writing business letters at her dictation, or reading aloud to her the reports of the various philanthropic, educational, or political institutions in which she was interested. She had been conscious on her arrival of a certain aloofness from her aunt's militant activities; but within a week she was swept back into the strong current of Mrs. Hayne's existence. It was like stepping from a gondola to an ocean steamer; at first she was dazed by the throb of the screw and the rush of parting waters, but gradually she felt herself infected by the exhilaration of getting to a fixed place in the shortest possible time. She could make sufficient allowance for the versatility of her moods to know that, a few weeks after her return to Paris, all that seemed most strenuous in Mrs. Hayne's occupations would fade to unreality; but that did not defend her from the strong spell of the moment. In its light her own life seemed vacuous, her husband's aim trivial as the subtleties of Chinese ivory carving; and she wondered if he walked in the same revealing flash.

Some three weeks after the arrival of the Corbetts in Mount Vernon Street, it became manifest that Mrs. Hayne had overtaxed her strength and must return for an undetermined period to her lounge. The life of restricted activity to which this necessity condemned her left her an occasional hour of leisure when there seemed no more letters to be dictated, no more reports to be read; and Corbett, always sure to do the right thing, was at hand to speed such unoccupied moments with the ready charm of his talk.

One day when, after sitting with her for some time, he departed to the club, Mrs. Hayne, turning to Delia, who came in to replace him, said, emphatically, "My dear, he's delightful."

"Oh, Aunt Mary, so are you!" burst gratefully from Mrs. Corbett.

Mrs. Hayne smiled. "Have you suspended your judgment of me until now?" she asked.

"No; but your liking each other seems to complete you both."

"Really, Delia, your husband couldn't have put that more gracefully; But sit down and tell me about him."

"Tell you about him?" repeated Delia, thinking of the voluminous letters in which she had enumerated to Mrs. Hayne the sum of her husband's merits.

"Yes," Mrs. Hayne continued, cutting, as she talked, the pages of a report on state lunatic asylums; "for instance, you've never told me why so charming an American has condemned America to the hard fate of being obliged to get on without him."

"You and he will never agree on that point, Aunt Mary," said Mrs. Corbett, coloring.

"Never mind; I rather like listening to reasons that I know beforehand I'm bound to disagree with; it saves so much mental effort. And besides, how can you tell? I'm very uncertain."

"You are very broad-minded, but you'll never understand his just having drifted into it. Any definite reason would seem to you better than that."

"Ah—he drifted into it?"

"Well, yes. You know his sister, who married the Comte de Vitrey and went to live in Paris, was very unhappy after her marriage; and when Laurence's mother died there was no one left to look after her; and so Laurence went abroad in order to be near her. After a few years Monsieur de Vitrey died too; but by that time Laurence didn't care to come back."

"Well," said Mrs. Hayne, "I see nothing so shocking in that. Your husband can gratify his tastes much more easily in Europe than in America; and, after all, that is what we're all secretly striving to do. I'm sure if there were more lunatic asylums and poorhouses and hospitals in Europe than there are here I should be very much inclined to go and live there myself."

Delia laughed. "I knew you would like Laurence," she said, with a wisdom bred of the event.

"Of course I like him; he's a liberal education. It's very interesting to study the determining motives in such a man's career. How old is your husband, Delia?"

"Laurence is fifty-two."

"And when did he go abroad to look after his sister?"

"Let me see—when he was about twenty-eight; it was in 1867, I think."

"And before that he had lived in America?"

"Yes, the greater part of the time."

"Then of course he was in the war?" Mrs. Hayne continued, laying down her pamphlet. "You've never told me about that. Did he see any active service?"

As she spoke Delia grew pale; for a moment she sat looking blankly at her aunt.

"I don't think he was in the war at all," she said at length in a low tone.

Mrs. Hayne stared at her. "Oh, you must be mistaken," she said, decidedly. "Why shouldn't he have been in the war? What else could he have been doing?"

Mrs. Corbett was silent. All the men of her family, all the men of her friends' families, had fought in the war; Mrs. Hayne's husband had been killed at Bull Run, and one of Delia's cousins at Gettysburg. Ever since she could remember it had been regarded as a matter of course by those about her that every man of her husband's generation who was neither lame, halt, nor blind should have fought in the war. Husbands had left their wives, fathers their children, young men their sweethearts, in answer to that summons; and those who had been deaf to it she had never heard designated by any name but one.

But all that had happened long ago; for years it had ceased to be a part of her consciousness. She had forgotten about the war; about her uncle who fell at Bull Run, and her cousin who was killed at Gettysburg. Now of a sudden, it all came back to her, and she asked herself the question which her aunt had just put to her—why had her husband not been in the war? What else could he have been doing?

But the very word, as she repeated it, struck her as incongruous; Corbett was a man who never did anything. His elaborate intellectual processes bore no flower of result; he simply *was*—but had she not hitherto found that sufficient? She rose from her seat, turning away from Mrs. Hayne.

"I really don't know," she said, coldly. "I never asked him."

IV

Two weeks later the Corbetts returned to Europe. Corbett had really been charmed with his visit, and had in fact shown a marked inclination to outstay the date originally fixed for their departure. But Delia was firm; she did not wish to remain in Boston. She acknowledged that she was sorry to leave her Aunt Mary; but she wanted to get home.

"You turncoat!" Corbett said, laughing. "Two months ago you reserved that sacred designation for Boston."

"One can't tell where it is until one tries," she answered, vaguely.

"You mean that you don't want to come back and live in Boston?"

"Oh, no—no!"

"Very well. But pray take note of the fact that I'm very sorry to leave. Under your Aunt Mary's tutelage I'm becoming a passionate patriot."

Delia turned away in silence. She was counting the moments which led to their departure. She longed with an unreasoning intensity to get away from it all; from the dreary house on Mount Vernon Street, with its stenciled hall and hideous drawing room, its monotonous food served in unappetizing profusion; from the rarefied atmosphere of philanthropy and reform which she had once found so invigorating; and most of all from the reproval of her aunt's altruistic activities. The recollection of her husband's delightful house in Paris, so framed for a noble leisure, seemed to mock the aesthetic barrenness of Mrs. Hayne's environment. Delia thought tenderly of the mellow bindings, the deep-piled rugs, the pictures, bronzes, and tapestries; of the "first nights: at the Francais, the eagerly discussed *conferences* on art or literature, the dreaming hours in galleries and museums, and all the delicate enjoyments of the life to which she was returning. It would be like passing from a hospital ward to a flower-filled drawing room; how could her husband linger on the threshold?

Corbett, who observed her attentively, noticed that a change had come over her during the last two weeks of their stay on Mount Vernon Street. He wondered uneasily if she were capricious; a man who has formed his own habits upon principles of the finest selection does not care to think that he has married a capricious woman. Then he reflected that the love of Paris is an insidious disease, breaking out when its victim least looks for it, and concluded that Delia was suffering from some such unexpected attack.

Delia certainly was suffering. Ever since Mrs. Hayne had asked her that innocent question—"Why shouldn't your husband have been in the war?"—she had been repeating it to herself day and night with the monotonous iteration of a monomaniac. Whenever Corbett came into the room, with that air of giving the simplest act its due value which made episodes of his entrances, she was tempted to cry out to him—"Why weren't you in the war?" When she heard him, at a dinner, point one of his polished epigrams, or smilingly demolish the syllogism of an antagonist, her pride in his achievement was chilled by the question—"Why wasn't he in the war?" When she saw him in the street, give a coin to a crossing sweeper, or lift his hat ceremoniously to one of Mrs. Hayne's maidservants (he was always considerate of poor people and servants) her approval winced under the reminder—"Why wasn't he in the war?" And when they were alone together, all through the spell of his talk and the exquisite pervasion of his presence ran the embittering undercurrent, "Why wasn't he in the war?"

At times she hated herself for the thought; it seemed a disloyalty to life's best gift. After all, what did it matter now? The war was over and forgotten; it was what the newspapers call "a dead issue." And why should any act of her husband's youth affect their present happiness together? Whatever he might once have been, he was perfect now; admirable in every relation of life; kind, generous, upright; a loyal friend, an accomplished gentleman, and, above all, the man she loved. Yes—but why had he not been in the war? And so began again the reiterant torment of the question. It rose up and lay down with her; it watched with her through sleepless nights, and followed her into the street; it mocked her from the eyes of strangers, and she dreaded lest her husband should read it in her own. In her saner moments she told herself that she was under the influence of a passing mood, which would vanish at the contact of her wonted life in Paris. She had become overstrung in the high air of Mrs. Hayne's moral enthusiasms; all she needed was to descend again to regions of more temperate virtue. This thought increased her impatience to be gone; and the days seemed interminable which divided her from departure.

The return to Paris, however, did not yield the hoped-for alleviation. The question was still with her, clamoring for a reply, and reinforced, with separation, by the increasing fear of her aunt's unspoken verdict. That shrewd woman had never again alluded to the subject of her brief colloquy with Delia; up to the moment of his farewell she had been unreservedly cordial to Corbett; but she was not the woman to palter with her convictions.

Delia knew what she must think; she knew what name, in the old days, Corbett would have gone by in her aunt's uncompromising circle.

Then came a flash of resistance—the heart's instinct of self-preservation. After all, what did she herself know of her husband's reasons for not being in the war? What right had she to set down to cowardice a course which might have been enforced by necessity, or dictated by unimpeachable motives? Why should she not put to him the question which she was perpetually asking herself? And not having done so, how dared she condemn him unheard?

A month or more passed in that torturing indecision. Corbett had returned with fresh zest to his accustomed way of life, weaned, by his first glimpse of the Champs Elysees, from his factitious enthusiasm for Boston. He and his wife entertained their friends delightfully, and frequented all the "first nights" and "private views" of the season, and Corbett continued to bring back knowing "bits" from the Hotel Drouot, and rare books from the quays; never had he appeared more cultivated, more decorative and enviable; people agreed that Delia Benson had been uncommonly clever to catch him.

One afternoon he returned later than usual from the club, and finding his wife alone in the drawing room, begged her for a cup of tea. Delia reflected, in complying, that she had never seen him look better; his fifty-two years sat upon him like a finish which made youth appear crude, and his voice, as he recounted his afternoon's doings, had the intimate inflections reserved for her ear.

"By the way," he said presently, as he set down his teacup, "I had almost forgotten that I've brought you a present—something I picked up in a little shop in the Rue Bonaparte. Oh, don't look too expectant; it's not a *chef-d'oeuvre*; on the contrary, it's about as bad as it can be. But you'll see presently why I bought it."

As he spoke he drew a small, flat parcel from the breast pocket of his impeccable frock coat and handed it to his wife.

Delia, loosening the paper which wrapped it, discovered within an oval frame studded with pearls and containing the crudely executed miniature of an unknown young man in the uniform of a United States cavalry officer. She glanced inquiringly at Corbett.

"Turn it over," he said.

She did so, and on the back, beneath two unfamiliar initials, read the brief inscription:

"Fell at Chancellorsville, May 3, 1863."

The blood rushed to her face as she stood gazing at the words.

"You see now why I bought it?" Corbett continued. "All the pieties of one's youth seemed to protest against leaving it in the clutches of a Jew pawnbroker in the Rue Bonaparte. It's awfully bad, isn't it?—but some poor soul might be glad to think that it had passed again into the possession of fellow countrymen." He took it back from her, bending to examine it critically. "What a daub!" he murmured. "I wonder who he was? Do you suppose that by taking a little trouble one might find out and restore it to his people?"

"I don't know—I dare say," she murmured, absently.

He looked up at the sound of her voice. "What's the matter, Delia? Don't you feel well?" he asked.

"Oh, yes. I was only thinking"—she took the miniature from his hand. "It was kind of you, Laurence, to buy this—it was like you."

"Thanks for the latter clause," he returned, smiling.

Delia stood staring at the vivid flesh tints of the young man who had fallen at Chancellorsville.

"You weren't very strong at his age, were you, Laurence? Weren't you often ill?" she asked.

Corbett gave her a surprised glanced. "Not that I'm aware of," he said; "I had the measles at twelve, but since then I've been unromantically robust."

"And you—you were in America until you came abroad to be with your sister?"

"Yes—barring a trip of a few weeks in Europe."

Delia looked again at the miniature; then she fixed her eyes upon her husband's.

"Then why weren't you in the war?" she said.

Corbett answered her gaze for a moment; then his lids dropped, and he shifted his position slightly.

"Really," he said, with a smile, "I don't think I know."

They were the very words which she had used in answering her aunt.

"You don't know?" she repeated, the question leaping out like an electric shock. "What do you mean when you say that you don't know?"

"Well—it all happened some time ago," he answered, still smiling, "and the truth is that I've completely forgotten the excellent reasons that I doubtless had at the time for remaining at home."

"Reasons for remaining at home? But there were none; every man of your age went to the war; no one stayed at home who wasn't lame, or blind, or deaf, or ill, or—" Her face blazed, her voice broke passionately.

Corbett looked at her with rising amazement.

"Or—?" he said.

"Or a coward," she flashed out. The miniature dropped from her hands, falling loudly on the polished floor.

The two confronted each other in silence; Corbett was very pale.

"I've told you," he said, at length. "That I was neither lame, deaf, blind, nor ill. Your classification is so simple that it will be easy for you to draw your own conclusion."

And very quietly, with that admirable air which always put him in the right, he walked out of the room. Delia, left alone, bent down and picked up the miniature; its protecting crystal had been broken by the fall. She pressed it close to her and burst into tears.

An hour later, of course, she went to ask her husband's forgiveness. As a woman of sense she could do no less; and her conduct had been so absurd that it was the more obviously pardonable. Corbett, as he kissed her hand, assured her that he had known it was only nervousness; and after dinner, during which he made himself exceptionally agreeable, he proposed their ending the evening at the Palais Royal, where a new play was being given.

Delia had undoubtedly behaved like a fool, and was prepared to do meet penance for her folly by submitting to the gentle sarcasm of her husband's pardon; but when the episode was over, and she realized that she had asked her questions and received her answer, she knew that she had passed a milestone in her existence. Corbett was perfectly charming; it was inevitable that he should go on being charming to the end of the chapter. It was equally inevitable that she should go on being in love with him; but her love had undergone a modification which the years were not to efface.

Formerly he had been to her like an unexplored country, full of bewitching surprises and recurrent revelations of wonder and beauty; now she had measured and mapped him, and knew beforehand the direction of every path she trod. His answer to her question had given her the clue to the labyrinth; knowing what he had once done, it seemed quite simple to forecast his future conduct. For that long-past action was still a part of his actual being; he had not outlived or disowned it; he had not even seen that it needed defending.

Her ideal of him was shivered like the crystal above the miniature of the warrior of Chancellorsville. She had the crystal replaced by a piece of clear glass which (as the jeweler pointed out to her) cost much less and looked equally well; and for the passionate worship which she had paid her husband she substituted a tolerant affection which possessed precisely the same advantages.

Brave Mrs. Lyle

Sarah B. Cooper

The heroism of common life finds little space in history. Of that more passive form of courage, called fortitude, which bears its burdens with a spirit steadfast and unbroken, the world takes small account. Like the air and sunlight, it pervades earth with an atmosphere of blessing, but is so generic in its scope as to be held cheap.

Champions of law and liberty, in Arkansas, had fallen upon troublous times. The Federal flotilla of gunboats, that swept down the Mississippi to aid in the Vicksburg struggle, virtually segregated the States west of the river; thus constituting a new department, more or less isolated in situation and circumscribed in action. General Foreman, once a representative of the State in the councilhalls of the nation, but now a zealous leader in the Confederate ranks, had returned to his native soil, and was enforcing a vigorous and ruthless conscription. Adherents to the Union cause, outside the pale of Federal protection, had learned to expect no quarter. Compelled allegiance to the rebel authorities, or the most bitter persecution—perhaps even death—these were the alternatives offered. There was no escape, except in stealthy flight. In counties more remote, lying west of the White River, affairs had assumed a perilous aspect. To be an avowed Unionist there, was to dare dangers the most imminent, and invite penalties the most appalling.

Nathaniel Lyle, a native of Pennsylvania, emigrated to Arkansas at an early day, and at the breaking out of the war was a well-to-do planter, in the western part of the State. A large inheritance of principle and pluck stood as atonement for meagre educational endowments; and these invaluable characteristics had been supplemented by that last best gift to man—a loving, sensible, heroic wife. But with the choice presented, of duty or trial, principle or persecution, there was no trembling hesitation, no weak dalliance: Mrs. Lyle knew what it was to suffer and be strong.

The solemn November day on which our story opens had been harsh and vexatious. The cows, at milking-time, had been perverse and vicious, completing a long catalogue of provoking peccadilloes with the final upsetting of a generous, well-filled milk-pail, wasting at once the product of their own day's scanty pickings, and the tired housewife's patient strippings. What made the matter far worse, was the fact that the milk had a special, predestined use. There was no mistake about it—this had been a day of marked disaster. Even the staid and decorous old plow-horses, Darby and Joan, whose historical record, in the matter of runaways, was without a blemish, had that morning, while coming down the long lane with a load of "lightwood," with evidently preconcerted action, pricked up their ears, caught the bit, and dashed down the road as if, contemptuous of humble pedigree, they would rival the proudest achievements of the best-bred Hambletonian.

This all-pervading, morbific tendency must have been atmospheric; else why should Charlie, the prince of good fellows, have lost his proverbial good-humor to such an extent as to declare that Nat, his baby brother, was a perfect little vixen, and to wonder what in the world he was ever made for, unless it was to "torment folks to death?" Sure enough, this was a problem that had puzzled wiser heads than Master Charlie's, since poor Mrs. Lyle had been going through such a sea of trouble.

It was almost midnight; Mrs. Lyle was still worrying with the despotic little tyrant Nat, who had maliciously set himself against sleep, and neither nursing, rocking, nor lullaby could budge him from his resolve. The other children—five, all told—had been sound asleep for three hours. Care-worn and very pale was that pleadingly-eloquent face, on which was recorded the story of an inevitable grief that she had hidden in the peaceful chambers of silence. Spirits sensitive, and finely strung, seem oft times to possess prophetic vision; they feel the shadow of coming calamity, even as we see the penumbra of an eclipse, that is to end in darkness. The exigency is upon her; there is no time for temporizing policies; desperate schemes are taking shape in her mind, as, with that pugnacious bit of babyhood tossed over her shoulder, she unconsciously rocks to and fro, keeping time to the sweet, mournful refrain with a pat on the back of the petty potentate. Poor little Nat was not in the least responsible for that mischievous sleeplessness and nervous disquietude. They were no less an inheritance from the sensitive, mettlesome mother, than were those large, brooding eyes, and soft brown curls, that set off his pretty baby face. Long before his name was added to the census-register of White County, or the air stirred with his first imperious cry, baby Nat had been in intimate sympathy with the troubled mother-heart, beneath which he lay enfolded. Wordsworth tells the story:

> *"Her little child*
> *Had from its mother caught the trick of grief,*
> *And sighed amid its playthings."*

The tall, old-fashioned clock in the corner struck the hour of midnight, and its harsh, metallic ring startled Mrs. Lyle to the consciousness of the pressing demands of the moment. Rising hastily, she laid the child, still broad awake, in his rustic, homespun crib, and proceeded to wrap herself in a coarse woolen cloak and hood, and taking from the closet a pair of strong boots, she drew them on, as if preparing for a long walk. Nat, who had been avenging himself for the indignity offered, by screaming at the top of his voice, had fairly worn himself out, and was snubbing and sobbing in the very dreariness of despair.

"No fresh milk for poor papa tonight," mused Mrs. Lyle, half-audibly, as she poured a panful from the morning's setting—cream and all—into a tin bucket, and placed it beside a large, well-filled basket, which stood near the door opening into the rear-yard.

Moving as quietly as her clumsy boots permitted, she approached the bed where Charlie lay sleeping—her first-born, noble boy, who, she repeatedly declared, was the greatest comfort a mother ever had. If baby Nat was a sadly-suggestive illustration of the baneful effects of an ante-natal atmosphere of sorrow and misfortune, Charlie was a triumphant exemplification of the salutary influence of pre-natal atmosphere of hope and joyful activity. It was no marvel that Charlie's whole being was absorbed in the prosperity and well-doing of his home, for he had been in closest sympathy with the buoyant efforts of the early wedded years which had established that home.

The sleeper murmured in his dreams, as the mother approached. "Come, Charlie," she said, softly, as she kissed his fair forehead—"come, my boy! I'm so sorry to disturb you; but Natty is so fretful to-night, and I must go to the camp, or your father will be caught by the conscript offi-cers, you know. They are on his track"—and she heaved a deep sigh, and uttered a brief ejaculatory prayer.

Charlie's ear caught both sigh and prayer, for he had slept as with one eye open for many a week, since the dangers thickened about them so fast.

"Yes, mother, I'll mind the baby; but hear the rain against the win-dows! Let me go and carry the things, and break the news. You can't cross the branch in such a storm as this."

"Yes, Charlie, I must go. I must see your father myself before he goes—God only knows where. Try and keep Natty from waking up the children; and mind that the fire don't fall down. I'll turn out the lamp, for the oil is nearly gone; but the light-wood fire will make it cheerful enough. Don't worry about me, Charlie."

With this, Mrs. Lyle packed up her burden, and glided noiselessly out into the darkness and storm. The load with which her hands wrestled was heavy enough; but the dull weight at her heart was far heavier. What was she to do? Whither should her husband flee to escape his persecutors? How could she protect herself and her children from the inevitable woes impending? A clap of thunder rent the air, and the wind shrieked and howled through the leafless trees—was this her answer? Perhaps, after the storm, would come the "still, small voice."

Mr. Lyle and a neighboring planter, Philip Nourse, had been "lying out" for nearly six weeks—fugitives from the infamous conscription so mercilessly enforced by Foreman. They were encamping in the woods about two miles off; hidden in a sort of natural fortress, formed by the convergence of hills, whose rugged sides offered at once protection and concealment. During all this time, Mrs. Lyle had been going twice every week with a supply of provisions and other little comforts, wherewith to cheer the exiles in their self-imposed but dreary banishment. These visitations were always made in the stillness and darkness of night; for the country was alive with spies, and discovery would bring disastrous, perhaps fatal consequences. What contributed no little to Mrs. Lyle's responsibility and burden, was the fact that her neighbor, Mrs. Nourse, was one of those dear, devoted little wives who know how to do nothing else, well, but to love and be loved in return—no mean accomplishments, but always the better for being reinforced with good, strong, womanly sense, and a *modicum,* at least of sterling executive talent. A hereditary predisposition to heart-disease had made Mr. Nourse all the more careful to shield his gentle wife from every possible hardship and annoyance. What with natural temperamental tendencies and the happiest experiences, Mrs. Nourse could be none other than she was—a veritable Griselda in loyal, trustful affection, but a tender-eyed Dora in helplessness and dependence. She was a child-wife. She wanted to be brave; but it was awkward business for her, in the absence of that great, manly breast upon which she was wont to pillow her drooping head. Poor Mrs. Nourse! She was doing wonders now, in caring for the blind sister, who was an inmate in the household; and keeping within bounds their only little boy, three years old and over, turbulent as he was with fresh young life—for the stir and vigor of the father was in him. Indeed, it is a question whether she would have gotten along at all, had not Mrs. Lyle, amidst her own over-burdening cares, managed to find opportunity to visit her every day, often assisting her in the very nick of time.

They had been waiting and watching for help from some quarter; they felt sure that relief would come—whence and how they hardly knew. But a new crisis had arisen. On the morning of the day in question, Charlie had been out in a deep thicket of second-growth pines, looking up stray cattle. Worn and exhausted with the tramp, he had thrown himself down in the underbrush, when the low hum of voices, not far off, caught his ear.

"There's no sort of doubt but they're hid out somewheres about here; for that plucky little woman wasn't coming in at that time o' night without some good reason for it. Why it must have been two o'clock in the morning, or better, when I saw her getting over the stile into the back yard. That was a lucky day for Nat Lyle, when he married Eunice Atherton. She's a deuced smart woman, and as good as she is smart."

"That's so, Cap; there wasn't another like her in Van Buren County. You didn't know I once set up to her myself, eh? But Nat got in ahead of me. I've never squared the account with him, yet; this may be my chance—who knows? But he's a devilish fine fellow, that Nat Lyle." The voice was deep-toned and resonant; but there was nothing vindictive in it.

Charlie hugged the ground still more closely, and listened breathlessly for the reply. After a moment's pause, the speaker continued: "I say, Cap, hadn't we better keep an eye on the little duck? Follow her, and we'll soon find out where the old drake is paddling. That's a pesky nice brood of ducklings—those Lyle young ones. The boy Charlie is his mother, right over again—quick as lightening and cunning as a fox. He's good grit, and no mistake. Why, that little cuss was born with more good sense than nine-tenths of folks die with. He's bound to make his mark some day—if somebody don't make a mark of him. If we can't do better, we can put some pretty straight questions to him. He's 'cute; but the sight of one of these 'tooth-picks' may fetch the secret out of him. He knows where his dad has vamosed to—no doubt of it!"

"But, Pete," the first speaker interposed, in a gruff, sepulchral tone, "you forget that we must down the valley to-night, and carry out the general's orders in regard to that blasted horse-stealing business, that he dignifies by the name of 'confiscation.' He says we'd better bring in no more miserable, broken-down animals like that old tackey which came so near costing him his life. Foreman is a catawamtious old cuss, and is getting a little too big for his boots. He'll get flipfloppussed himself before he knows it. I'm getting deuced tired of his nonsense. He's too durned cruel to suit my notion of things. He walks into folks too rough, altogether. Lyle and Nourse have got a lot of choice blooded stock, that they set great store by; and the orders are, to take the last one of them—drive the cattle down the river—unearth the men-folks and press them into service, or burn their old shebangs to the ground. Now, that's devilish rough on the women folks, just as winter's setting in! But the old moke won't rest till it's done. I reckon Bill's right about it—the old skeezicks means to kill off Lyle, and marry the widow himself."

"Reckon he'll slip up on that," returned Pete, a little flushed. "The general won't do to tie to in such matters, anyhow. But I allow, we'd better do one thing or t'other—either turn tail on the old slang-whanger altogether, or else rope in, and obey orders. You know, Cap, the general on you as the bell-mare of us skalawags; you mustn't play out. I hate this sneak-thief sort of business as much as you do. These poor fellows have worked for what they have got, and it's tight on 'em. Speaking of blooded stock, Cap, reminds me of that colt, Nebo, that old man Atherton gave Charlie for his name. Why, the boy fairly worships the animal; and he's as pretty a piece of horseflesh as I ever laid eyes on. It's astonishing to see the tricks the boy has taught him. They understand each other better than we do. Some animals are half-human, I believe. Charlie declares Nebo will do wonders one o'these days. 'Taint worth while to pester the child's colt, whatever else we take. Let the boy have him. Besides, he's like half the women-folks, nowadays—more for show than good hard work. We'd better let the colt alone."

Charlie bristled at the thought of Nebo's danger, and instinctively sprang to his feet. It was well for him that just at that instant the two men moved toward their horses, browsing in an opposite direction. Discretion mastered emotion, and Charlie dropped down again into the pine straw, and laid concealed in the thick underbrush. As the riders dashed by, within a few feet, he caught the words, "We must get back by day after to-morrow, and follow the little partridge to the ambush."

Here was a revelation, the full significance of which Mrs. Lyle was prepared to grasp, as Charlie—all alive with excitement—detailed the marvelous disclosure. It was evident that her movements had been watched; that her husband's retreat would be discovered; that she herself might be forced to reveal it; and that he would be at their mercy unless she went, at once, to tell him the whole story, and hasten him forward to the Federal lines. To know that the marauders were to be gone down the valley for two days, re-assured her for the struggle. It was a comfort, too, to feel that a latent spark of humanhood still lingered in the breasts of the desperate men with whom she must sooner or later deal, and who so largely controlled her destiny. Could it be possible that Peter Preston, who, years ago, when she was a mere school-girl, talked so softly and sweetly to her, under the big magnolia, in her father's garden—could it be that he would harm her now, in her helplessness and desolation? She could not believe it. She had too much faith in manhood. She had too much trust in heaven. He might feel bound to obey the orders of his superior officer, but, in carrying them out, he would not insult and abuse her, or her children. The thought consoled her, as she struggled on through the darkness and storm to the rescue of her husband.

Drenched to the skin, and too much exhausted even to speak, Mrs. Lyle reached the camp of the fugitives—a rude inclosure, improvised of pine boughs and alien remnants of a railfence, that had been dragged for more than a mile. She fell prostrate as she reached the door of the cabin. It was a perilous and dreary scene. The lightning flashed with a glare that illumined the woods with floods of flame; thunder on thunder rent the air; rain poured in torrents from each gathering cloud; streams dashed along the deluged valley, and the crest of the surging waters seemed tipped with fire; wind howled to wind, through the swaying trees; the heavens scowled, and Nature was draped in the garniture of woe. The scene without was a fitting accompaniment to the recital within; although Mrs. Lyle, in hurrying preparations for their immediate departure, took good care to represent all home affairs in *couleur de rose*, as far as possible. They needed the tonic of a brave nature like hers in this terrible exigency. Many a man, lacking it, at such a crisis, has irrevocably fallen.

But we turn to the scene at home. Mrs. Lyle had been gone less than a half-hour, when a fearful clap of thunder startled Nat from his troubled sleep, and he sent up at once an imprecating psalm. Charlie was hushing him to quietude, by pacing back and forth across the room in the soft glimmer of the light-wood fire. A momentary lull in the storm revealed the approach of hurrying footsteps, followed by a quick rap on the back-door. The branch was doubtless impassable, and his mother had been compelled to return. Charlie stepped nimbly, and turned back the clumsy bolt, when the two men whom he had seen in the thicket presented themselves, in evident disguise.

"Pretty late for young chaps like you to be up. Where's all the folks?"

If there had been a doubt as to the *personnel* of the speaker, there could be no mistaking that voice. It was the dull, stentorian drawl of Cap; Charlie knew it at once, and his mother-wit indicated the answer.

"Why, father he's been gone for six weeks, or better; and mother she's been going down the valley to Mrs. Haley's, every chance she could get, for a fortnight. They've got a new baby down there—he's a cripple—and they're afraid Mrs. Haley aint going to get well."

"So your mother's down to old Haley's, is she?" (Charlie had not said so; but no commandment had been broken.) "And your dad—where's he, p'rhaps?"

"Perhaps he's in the Federal lines, by this time," responded Charlie, repeating the adverb with concealed but grateful satisfaction. "That's the safest place for folks to be these days. But won't you come in and dry yourselves? I'll chuck on some fat knots, and have a scorcher in a jiffy. It's pouring down faster than ever. You'd better come in."

There was a childish welcome in the invitation, and a trustful frankness that softened the heart of the interrogator, who replied: "No, thank you; we wanted to see your father. What time d'ye reckon your mother'll be back?"

"By late milking-time in the morning, for nobody else can manage the little red heifer; she's like Natty (giving the baby fresh prominence), nobody but mother can do anything with her."

Pete, who had not spoken during the interview, turned on his heel, saying, "Come, let's be off!" and the two disappeared in the darkness.

Long before daylight, drenched and dripping in front of the fire, Mrs. Lyle was listening to the story of the unexpected *denouement*. The terrible storm had doubtless prevented their contemplated trip down the valley. The crisis was upon her. There was no time for delay. The twilight of the morning found her tapping softly at the window of Mrs. Nourse, awakening her from a heavy slumber. No rude, nocturnal visitors had disturbed her sleep; for this she was thankful, not alone for her own sake, for if the child-wife had been taken unawares, she might, in her weak fear, have disclosed everything. She must be fortified against attack.

Mrs. Nourse took in the significance of the situation much after the manner of a child. She realized there was a great volume of wretchedness, but of the contents-table of detail she took not the slightest account. "What *must* I do?" she asked, with pleading entreaty.

"Just say the men have gone to the Federal lines, and stick to it. Don't let them get another word out of you! Federal lines—Federal lines! do you understand?"

"Oh, yes; I understand. I won't say another word, if they choke me." And the flushed and purple face looked as if the process of choking had already begun.

"Now give me your valuable papers and keepsakes," continued Mrs. Lyle. "I will put them in a stone jar with my own, and bury them in the cave. Be quick! If anything happens, leave little Phil with Rachel, and run over to me."

Poor Rachel! had she been deaf as well as blind, she might have been spared the agony she was now suffering.

The storm had abated. The sun was struggling through the falling mist, and far up the blue sky the rainbow arch appeared, as if angelic watchers, in the plenitude of sympathetic love, had bent over the pearly battlements to unfold the covenant pledge of heaven to weary, overspent mortals. Mrs. Lyle interpreted the full meaning of the soft-tinted emblem, and was refreshed for duty.

It was not far from noon when four horsemen appeared at the gate. One of them dismounted and presented himself at the door. There was a blended air of affected civility and saucy bluntness in manner and speech.

"We take it you know something of your old man's whereabouts these days. If you'll be good enough to mount one o'these animals at the gate and lead the way, you shan't be harmed."

Argument would be wasted. Numbers might prove her protection. In any event, she would rather accept the risks than imperil Mrs. Nourse. She stepped to the gate to see if Pete was of the party. His disguise did not conceal his identity, but it was a secret all her own. Looking him full in the eye, she said: "I'm not afraid to trust that face. I will go with you where I last met my husband, although I assure you he is now seeking Federal protection; he is no longer there. You will let me ride a horse that better suits me, I'm sure. Here, Charlie, saddle Nebo, and bring him to the door!"

The men were awestruck and confounded; they did not interpose a word. The imperial majesty of her exalted womanhood had subdued and overmastered them. They were her subjects; she was not their slave. The omnipotence of her sublime heroism compelled their worship.

The companionship of a trusty brute, in such peril, is a solace; there is conscious sympathy. Through bog and *debris* Nebo daintily picked his way, obedient to the firm rein of his well-known rider, whose thoughts just now far outdistanced his constrained pace. Mrs. Lyle was in no hurry. Every minute increased the distance between the pursued and the pursuers—at least, she hoped so. But what if the streams beyond had forced them to return? What if the storm had shut out all hope of escape? Once or twice she was startled by the sound of her own voice, as she mused. Had they overheard her fears? They were following at a distance, mute and respectful.

The camp was now in sight. There was no smoke, no appearance of life. A moment more and it proved itself deserted. Mrs. Lyle thought she detected a glint of satisfaction on Pete's face. Possibly she was mistaken, but it emboldened her to say: "You see it is just as I told you. Here is where

I used to bring food to them, but they have gone to the Federal lines."

A few words, but not of censure, and the riders put spurs to their horses and dashed off toward the river. They would not be likely to surprise the fugitives, for their route lay in the opposite direction.

Perilous days followed. Rumors of devastation reached them from every quarter. They were in constant dread of a similar fate. In the dim twilight of an evening, early in December, a horseman, riding furiously down the road, darted up to the back-gate, and, throwing a package quite into the small piazza, disappeared in the bushes. Charlie, who caught a glimpse of the rider, declared him to be Pete Preston. The contents of the envelope gave confirmation of his statement. The note was bried, and ran thus:

> "Danger is at hand. Brave as you are, you can not cope
> with rapine, fire, and exposure. Those who would help
> you are powerless to do so. Flee at once to Federal pro-
> tection, and delay not a moment."

To a nature less resolute this would have been an hour unredeemed by hope; but Mrs. Lyle's unflagging vigor kept her activities abreast of her quick, intuitive plans, and the magnetic influence of her undaunted courage would have inspired the veriest coward with confidence. What was this but genius?

The old clock struck three, and Mrs. Lyle was still busy with hasty preparations for departure. She must, if possible, snatch a few moments' rest, and then lend assistance to her faint-hearted neighbor, who was to go with them. But there was no truce to be made with sleep; a vision of disaster usurped the place of slumber. Was it the stir of trouble from without, or the mute prophecy of doom from within? The solution of the problem was at hand. A flash of light from across the way told the story. Mrs. Nourse's dwelling was in flames, and, wild with terror, the half-crazed inmates were fleeing up the road toward Mrs. Lyle's.

"They've burned us up! They've burned us up!" shrieked the frantic woman, clutching her boy with one hand, and poor, blind Rachel with the other. "What shall we do—what shall we do? You'll go next!"

With the air of one accustomed to command, this mother-generalis-
simo hurried forward preparations for immediate flight. Was she to be
foiled at the very first step? A visit to the stable found every stall empty;
not a horse remained—not even Nebo. To resolve was to do. Two stout
yoke of oxen were still available. They had done generous duty in front of
the great lumbering country-wagon for many a year. An ample commis-
sariat and plenty of warm blankets and other little comforts were hurriedly stowed away within its great, swelling sides, and, before noon, the heavy-
laden, heavy-hearted emigrant train was under way for Memphis—more
than a hundred miles distant—over a rough, unfrequented route, and in
midwinter ofttimes impassable.

Family-life in a country-wagon, with a party of ten, including seven
children, a blind dependent, a weak, fragile woman, exhausted with fatigue
and fright, and a turbulent little autocrat like Nat, was calculated to test the
mettle of the hardiest campaigner. In Charlie, her second-self, Mrs. Lyle
found strength and cheer. His innate manhood expanded with the emer-
gency. The third morning rose on a scene of fresh and unlooked-for sorrow. Mrs. Nourse, who seemed to be sleeping later than usual, was found
to be dead. She had slipped away in the shadows of night, and had gone
home, leaving to her little boy, who lay enfolded in her cold arms, the sweet
legacy of a smile.

A hushed, funereal sadness lingered about the journeyers all that dreary day, as the great clumsy wagon, at once their hearse and home, dragged
on through marsh and lagoon, till toward sunset a hint of habitation
appeared in view; when kindly hands assisted in a hasty burial, and twilight
dews shed holy tears over the new-made grave of the pilgrim—at rest.

Three weeks of wearisome journeying through dangerous defiles and over
rugged corduroy roads and we find the refugees—ten, less one—sharing the
hospitality of a genial-souled planter—though southern in sentiment, yet warm
of heart—who, coming upon the strange group around their evening camp-
fire, and learning something of their history, insisted upon their occupying
some vacant cabins in his own yard. They had crossed the river, and were within five miles of Memphis. A few days of rest would better prepare them for

whatever of struggle awaited them there.

But misfortune had his iron grip upon them—they were fairly at bay with fate. Sudden and serious illness fell upon the planter, which physicians pronounced to be a malignant form of measles, prevalent in the army encamped all about, and frequently fatal. To expose her family to this, was to invite further disaster; for not one of them had ever had the contagious disease.

With a small amount of means—the proceeds of the sale of her oxen to the planter, who was disposed to afford her all the aid in his power— she managed to get through the lines, and make her way into the city. It was not difficult to secure temporary protection; and prospects were encouraging for obtaining a meagre subsistence.

But her stay at the planter's, brief as it had been, was to have its sad sequel. The mother was the first to succumb to the insidious disease, leaving her family helpless. Her case was quickly made known to "The Society for the Protection of Refugees," then in active operation in Memphis, and a home was provided for her in the refugee hospital. Every member of the family was ill—three dangerously so. Blind Rachel was the first to be carried to Elmwood—the darkness of earth had given place to the brightness of heaven. A few days, and little Nat followed—going up to the better nursery of angels. The rest, save Charlie, were doing well.

Poor Mrs. Lyle! She was slowly recovering; and Charlie's critical condition left no time for useless repinings. A council of physicians had pronounced his case hopeless; but the mother still clung to her boy with a grasp that would not let him go—with an agonizing faith that cried, "Though he slay me, yet will I trust in him."

All was hushed in the darkened wards of the hospital. Sleep had fallen upon most of its inmates. Stillness reigned, broken only, at times, by the troubled groan of tossing patients, who were perhaps dreaming of home, and friends far away. Charlie laid quiet, almost breathless, in his unconsciousness. Mrs. Lyle, agonized and tearful, yet still clinging to a desperate hope, sat by his bedside, holding on her lap little Phil Nourse, whom she was trying to soothe and comfort in his feverish fretfulness. That pale

mother-face, lying back in the valley, was ever pleadingly before her, and
the orphan boy was her tender care. Sitting in the mournful silence, the
events of the past few weeks flitted in dreary succession before her. She
was almost paralyzed with grief. Charlie gave a sudden start, and, looking
wildly about him for a moment, shrieked aloud the name of "mother!"
and, sinking back, was as one dead. Was this, then, the final blow? She
uttered a pleading cry, stroked his cold forehead, hugged the orphan baby
still more closely to her heart, and sank back in a swoon.

> *"Then whisper'd the angel of mothers*
> *To the watcher, in gentle tone,*
> *'One so kind to the children of others*
> *Doth richly deserve her own.'"*

Charlie was given back to her, as one alive from the dead. The blackened
cloud began to unfold its silver lining.

Ministering often ends in being ministered unto. Bread cast upon the
waters is sure to find its way back, after many days. Winter had given place
to spring, and Mrs. Lyle, with her family (now reduced to seven members),
was anchored again at the homestead of the planter, who had, so unwit-
tingly, bequeathed her such a heritage of woe. His house had once been
her protection—she was now to be its defense. His own sickness had
proved fatal; and Mrs. Lyle had been sought out by the widow, to afford at
the same time fellowship and security. Smuggled goods, for the
Confederacy, had been discovered secreted about the place; and, although
consciously innocent herself, her property was threatened with confiscation. By her trials and persecutions, Mrs. Lyle had become well known to
the Federal authorities, who were disposed to render her generous assistance. Her presence at the plantation would insure its safety. The offer of
the widow was munificent: liberal provision for all her family wants—supplies for the needed plantation hands—the entire jurisdiction of the place,
and an equal share in the crop. With the details of cotton-raising she was
amply familiar; a good overseer was already on the spot; and, being so near
the city, colored help was not difficult to secure. Even the patient oxen

seemed to catch, instinctively, the situation of affairs, and bent eagerly to their task, as if ambitious of doing their part in replenishing an impoverished family exchequer. The heavens were propitious with sunshine and rain, and an abundant crop rewarded patient toil.

A single notable incident enlivened the dull monotone of daily plantation life. Charlie had gone to town on some household commission, and was passing down a frequented street where a quartermaster's sale of condemned stock was going on. A man emerged from the crowd leading a fleet-limbed animal, with glossy mane and flowing tail, and a neck still proudly arched, though spurs had seamed and scarred his lean, weather-beaten sides, and the significant "I. C." flared ignominiously from his shapely flank.

"There's Nebo!" shouted Charlie; and, with a bound, he sprang to the side of the animal. "That's my colt, sir—my colt!"—and his face flushed with a joyful excitement that gave full attestation to the assertion.

"Your colt?—the deuce it is! Why, I've just planked fifty dollars for him. Don't you see that?"—pointing to the hateful brand.

"O yes; I see! But won't you let me talk a bit to the colt, and I'll show you he was mine. He was stolen, sir—stolen over in White County. Here, Nebo!" and Charlie proffered a lump of sugar, which he had taken from a package on his arm. At the sound of his name, the animal pricked up his ears in a knowing way, and his flashing eye kindled with a new fire. Charlie patted him caressingly, as he repeated the question: "I say, Nebo! do you want this lump of sugar? If you do, up with your white foot!"

With a sniff of recognition, Nebo lifted the dainty limb, once so supple, but now perceptibly stiffened with hard usage, yet still awkwardly obedient to the behests of its young trainer. Without a word of protest, the generous dealer placed the halter in Charlie's hand, saying, "Here, my boy! take your colt; you well deserve it. I'm no stranger to horses; but that beats all, in the way of horse-sense, that I ever saw." Charlie once prophesied that Nebo would do wonders, yet; the prediction was likely to be fulfilled.

A year had elapsed since their exodus from home; still, no tidings of the fugitives, although letters and messages had been dispatched in every direction. They were undoubtedly dead. Hardship and exposure, or the hand of the assassin, had accomplished the work. It was the anniversary of that dreadful December day, which, opening in conflagrations, found every stall empty, and the rude ox-team their *dernier ressort* for flight. Mrs. Lyle and the widow had been in town all day, purchasing a stock of winter supplies. It was the dusk of evening, and they were slowly approaching home. Mrs. Lyle's thoughts were busy with the past. Nebo, who was in front of the carryall , was doing his best, but showed evident signs of fatigue;—the roads were heavy, and his wonted vigor had not yet returned. Two men, suddenly emerging from a by-path, eyed them with a scrutiny well calculated to awaken suspicion and alarm. Their gaze seemed riveted on Nebo, who, just now, was tugging heroically with the deep ruts of the road. Through the increasing darkness, the shadowy outlines of figures were but dimly visible. They drew near, as if to seize the bridle.

"What do you want?" Mrs. Lyle's voice was firm and commanding in emphasis; but the music of its tone was not to be disguised—it disclosed its ownership.

"Want? why we want *you*, my precious wife! God be praised, we have found you at last!"

But the woman at her side was not Mrs. Nourse. For *him*, the comrade of the speaker, there remained a mournful recital, which was the grave of hope.

The story of the wanderers is soon told. They had reached the Federal lines—enlisted in the Union service—fought in many a battle—been shut up in hospital from sickness and wounds; and, obtaining a furlough at the first opportunity , had hurried back to their homes, to find nothing but desolation—not a house remaining. Not a trace of their families could be discovered. Their route had been eastward—this was all they could learn. Reaching Memphis, they had obtained a clue to their whereabouts, and were prosecuting the search when Nebo presented himself, and was instantly recognized. Verily, he had "done wonders!"

Peace had once more unfolded her fair pinions over a distracted land. The exiles had returned to their homes, beyond the White River. The product of the cotton crop sufficed to rebuild the Lyle farm-house. But poor Philip Nourse—what had he? A few acres of overgrown, neglected land—a share in the contents of the unmolested stone jar, buried in the cave—little Phil, well kept and rosy-cheeked, a perpetual reminder of one gone—a stranded and bitter spirit: these were all that remained to him. There was not even a mound on the hillside to tell of the sweet and loving child-wife.

A protracted civil war leaves many claims for adjustment. Unhappily they are not all of a monetary nature. Vengeance, deep-brooding over dire cruelty, sometimes refuses to sheathe the blood-stained sword.

Foreman had returned unharmed to his native soil, and to the practice of his profession. His legal acumen, however, did not avail to protect him from a stray bullet that went whizzing through the open window of his dwelling, to find a lodgment in his heart. If sent in retribution by a foe, he was never discovered; and efforts to unearth him were not gigantic.

During their long banishment, Charlie had made numerous friends, both in the army and outside. Among the former were those who insisted that he should be fortified against possible future exigencies, by a thorough education at the expense of the Government, in one of the first military schools of the country.

"Go! my dear boy," said Mrs. Lyle. "Your country may need your best service, by and by; and Nebo may yet 'do wonders' as your war-horse—who can tell? But Heaven forbid that you should ever ride forth to the dreadful conflicts of another civil war!"

From A Soldier's Wife

Bella Z. Spencer

At Paducah, Kentucky, I first realized what it required to be a soldier's wife. I had seen much before, and borne a great deal, yet it seemed but little comparatively when I came to take leave of my husband, and turned back to my lonely room to await his return.

True, I had expected this—was prepared for it in a measure; yet a strange and overpowering sense of my position came over me that I had not felt before, when I stood by the window to catch a last glimpse of a beloved form. He was standing upon the deck of a large boat, with hundreds of others around him; yet I seemed to see him only, his sad face turned to me in a mute farewell as the bell clanged and the ponderous vessel swept slowly out into the stream, and turned her prow toward the mouth of the Tennessee. It was but a moment, during which I leaned against the casement, breathless, agonized. There the waters lay cold and glittering under the spring sunbeams, and the sadness of utter desolation seemed to have fallen upon my spirits.

I am ashamed to say that I shut every ray of the bright, beautiful sun from my room, feeling as if it was a mockery too bitter to endure in that hour; that I threw myself upon my couch and wept as if my heart would break, for the time forgetful that there were any in the world more sorrowful, and with deeper cause for sorrow than I. But it is true, and here I confess my selfish weakness repentantly, glad to be able to say that I have since that time learned to think less of myself and more of others on whom the hand of affliction has fallen heavily, while I am still unscathed.

After the first burst of grief I roused myself with the question, "What shall I do?"and the answer came so quickly that my cheek was dyed with shame. What should I do, with three hospitals in sight of my window? No need to ponder the question long. The call of duty was loud and strong, and I obeyed it without delay.

It was about two o'clock in the afternoon when I first entered the Presbyterian church, which had been converted into a hospital, and walked up its aisle under the gaze of a hundred eyes. The very remembrance of that time thrills me again with the same sensation of pity and pain that rose in my heart as I looked upon the pale, emaciated faces around me. Near the pulpit two men were standing, whom I rightly supposed to be the doctor and steward. Toward them I went directly, and addressed the tallest of the two.

"Is this the attending physician of the hospital?"

"It is, madam. Dr. L—, at your service. What can I do for you?"

"Tell me, Sir, how I can make myself useful to others. My husband has gone to Pittsburg Landing, to be away for several weeks, perhaps, during which time I shall have nothing to do, unless you make me useful here. Can I be of service?"

"Look around you and see. There has not been a lady here within these walls since I came, nearly five weeks ago. Your voice is soft, your hand light and skillful—all women's are—and I have no doubt but your eyes will be quick to see what should be done. I shall be glad to have you come."

"Thank you. I may come to you for advice when I want it?" I asked.

"Certainly. I shall be happy to assist you at all times."

I bowed and turned away, feeling as if about to realize, indeed, some of the terrible consequences of war.

In a few moments I had laid aside my hat and cloak, rolled my sleeves away from my wrists, and constructed an impromptu apron of an old sheet which I found among the bandages in the linen room. Thus prepared for the work which I saw before me, I went out to the kitchen and obtained warm water, a tin wash-basin, and some towels. For combs and brushes I was compelled to send out before I could do any thing.

Then the work began in earnest. Commencing with the lower berth, I went up the entire length of the aisle, taking each patient in his turn until I got through. Grimed faces and hands were to be bathed, hair and beard trimmed and brushed—a long and distressing task. But I had undertaken it with a will, and, though my arms and neck ached, I would not yield until the last sufferer had been relieved.

It was half past eight o'clock in the evening before I had done, and when I reached the hotel I could scarcely stand for very weariness. Such duties were new to me then, and the excitement helped to wear away my strength. But the memory of grateful thanks, tearful eyes, and broken, trembling exclamations of relief more than repaid me. Even as I sat beside them, passing the cool sponge over their faces or brushing the tangled hair, many of the sufferers had fallen asleep.

I slept little that night. It was vain attempt to sleep after such an experience. Moreover, an idea came to me that filled me with unrest. I had observed when tea was brought in how coarse and unpalatable the food was, and that many turned from it with loathing. There was hard, brown bread crisped to a blackened toast; some fat bacon, and black tea without milk served to the men on that evening. The tea was sweetened with very coarse brown sugar, stirred into it with large iron spoons. They drank from tin cups and ate from tin plates. This would have made little difference had the food been nice and palatable, which it certainly was not. Some of the men told me, in answer to my questions, that they could not have swallowed a mouthful to save their lives.

I rose very early the following morning, filled with the idea that many of those brave sufferers were actually starving, and determined to look into the matter more closely. But few of the nurses were astir in the hospital, and I went to the kitchen, where the cook had just commenced the preparation of the morning meal, and was greeted with a surly "Good-morgen" in mixed German-English. In a moment I saw that I should not have a very pleasant time in my examinations. After a few careless remarks, to set the man in a good-humor, I asked him to show me the hospital stores for the day's consumption, which he did ungraciously enough. A moment's observation filled me with horror and indignation.

"Do you tell me that you are going to cook all this stuff for those men in the other room?" I said, indignantly. "Look at this tea, black and mouldy as it can be, and this bacon is one living mass! Here are salt fish laid upon boards over the sugar-barrel, brine dripping through into the sugar! I hope you have not been using this for their tea."

"It is not my fault. I am not ze prowider fur ze hospital," growled the cook in response. "I does my duty so fur as I can. I cooks ze rations zat is bring to me, and zat is all so fur as I go."

"Well, that is farther that you will go in less than a week from now!" I answered, quickly. "If you had the soul of a man in you, you would refuse to have any thing to do with such horrible things as those! Poor boys! No wonder they turned away from such food in disgust. Some of those men are starving to death. Do you know it?"

He stared at me aghast and made no reply.

"It is really true, and I know it. How can they eat such bread and meat—drink such tea as this? They are weakened by illness, and require delicacies. It would be utterly impossible for many of those men to swallow coarse food, even if clear and palatable. How then can they eat this?" I repeated, looking at him steadily till his head drooped, and I began to suspect that he was even more guilty than he at first appeared. Afterward I found that he had carefully put aside all the delicacies that found their way to the hospital and feasted upon them, while those for whom they were intended faded and pined day by day under his eyes.

When Dr. L— came I went to him at once and told him how I had been engaged, and what I had found in my researches. He looked so much surprised that indignation was redoubled, and I could not forbear expressing it in plain words.

"Can it be possible that you, the physician in charge of a hospital, do not know, after five weeks' service, what your patients have to eat?"

"I am not here when the meals are served. I give orders for such diet as my patients must have, and my steward's business is to carry out my instructions."

"Do you never inquire into the condition of the stores? Have you never examined to see if they were as they should be? It seems to me you ought to know what is going on here. If three hundred lives were in my hands as they are in yours I should not dare to trifle with them thus!"

"You are severe, madam!"

"Ask yourself if I am unjustly so, Sir. I do not desire to appear rude or assuming; but indeed I won't look upon this unmoved. What I saw last night and this morning has opened my eyes to a condition that is a shame to any hospital. See the confusion all around us! Remember how long the helpless men have lain without even a face bath or a wound dressed for three days, to say nothing of the more dreadful slow starvation to which they are subjected! If all hospitals are kept like this God pity the poor soldiers!"

"Since you see the evils so plainly, perhaps you can suggest a remedy," remarked Dr. L——, sarcastically.

"I will try, if you will act upon the suggestion," I answered, quickly.

"Well?"

"In the first place, then, what do you do when a man fails to draw his regular rations?"

"He is entitled to its value in money if he wishes it."

"Then why not refuse to draw such rations as those, and with the money buy food that can be eaten?"

"It might be done if there was any thing to buy. I am afraid it will be hard work it you attempt it."

"No matter; it must be done. If you will furnish me with a boy to do errands, I will see if I can not get fresh butter, eggs, and chickens, at least—perhaps milk also. These would prove invaluable just now. To-day I intend to send to a Society for some sheets and mattresses; and, if you have no decided objection, will try to bring order out of chaos, if possible."

"I see you are one of the working kind," said the Doctor. "Do all you wish, and call upon me when I can render any assistance."

"That will be very frequently, I assure you." And with that I turned away, still too much incensed to treat him civily. He was willing enough to let other people take his work off his hands, since he would come in for a full share of the credit in the end. At least that was my uncharitable thought at the moment; and I am not sure now that I was far wrong, as I know his character better.

The same day I went to him again about the boy, but he had forgotten all about the matter, so I went to the Quarter-master instead. He furnished a horse, and I sent my own waiting-man out to the country for supplies, making him take a receipt for every penny he paid in his purchases. This was for the purpose of ascertaining precisely how much was spent, as I desired to render a faithful account of my stewardship. I was fully aware that the ground I was taking might easily prove a dangerous one should I fail to keep precise accounts of my expenditures, and resolved to give no chances for misrepresentation. Every receipt and bill of sale, after being duly copied in my own account-book, was carefully filed in the Quarter-master's office, subject to the inspection of any who chose to examine them.

Mr. P——, the Quarter-master, was a kind, gentlemanly man, in whom I found an ever-ready assistant. He had received a donation in money, for the benefit of the wounded, from some one in Illinois, which he begged me to use as designed, and I did so gladly. Even with that I had not enough, and was often compelled to draw from my own purse the means wherewith to supply the many wants of the patients.

It took me a week to get fairly started in my vocation as hospital nurse. There was such an entire absence of system in the establishment, that it seemed almost impossible to bring it into any thing like order. The nurses were detailed each day from the convalescent corps—weak, spiritless men, who thought more of themselves than of the charges placed in their hands. I had seen them lounging about and sleeping while the sicker men, failing to make them hear, would try to struggle into a sitting position to get at the medicines to be taken from time to time.

All this had to be changed, and strong, able men detailed for duty. The ward-master drank fearfully, and I was compelled to report him and get another man put into his place. With the assistance of these, however, after changes were made I got along very well. Every morning we had the floor nicely washed, and when the sun shone the windows were opened to let in the fresh, balmy air, the effect of which was almost magical; eyes would brighten, and lips wreathe in pleasant, hopeful smiles, beautiful to behold.

It was with more joy than words can express that I observed the rapid improvement of the men under careful attention. When the new sheets and comforters, with pillows and mattresses came, we were able to keep the place perfectly fresh and comfortable. But it required the most constant attention. I went to my hotel only for my meals, devoting the day, from half past five in the morning to nine in the evening, to the care of the sick. I must be there at every meal, or many would go without any thing at all. Some of the feeblest had to be fed like children, and what they ate must be prepared by myself only. I must toast the bread and make the tea; then I must sit down and support their heads with my left hand , while with the right I conveyed the food to their lips. Such constant care was very wearing, and I was often tempted to steal away for an hour's rest, trusting to some one to take my place for a time; but when I gave it a second thought the temptation faded. Suppose the man should die, could I feel that I had done all in my power to save him? Not if I should yield to the inclination I felt to abandon my post; so I remained, and tried to be patient.

Two hours each day were devoted to letter-writing for those who were unable to correspond with their friends. And sometimes, after tea, I would send for my guitar and sing for them, at the request of the music-loving ones under my charge. So the days sped, and all things began to run smoothly—for a time, at least. Death was not banished from our midst, however. Sometimes it was my fate to walk up the aisle in the morning and find some berth empty in which a favorite patient had lain. I might here go into particulars, and detail some of the most touching scenes in life; but I will here speak of only one case:

One evening I was sitting by a dying man, reading a favorite chapter in the Bible, to which he listened eagerly, even while his eyes drooped under the shades of death. One clammy hand groped for mine, and clasped it with a feeble, tremulous touch, and as I finished his lips moved painfully: "Write to my wife and children. Tell them I can not come to them, but they may soon follow me to that place of which the Savior said, 'In my Father's house are many mansions: I go to prepare a place for you.' Oh, how sweet and comforting! 'Let not your hearts be troubled: ye who believe in God; believe also in me.' Jesus Savior, I do believe in thee. Receive my spirit!" And the voice sank softly. A few moments later the last fluttering breath went out, and the mysteries of the unknown world were mysteries to him no longer.

Tears fell fast as I pressed the white lids over the blue eyes, thinking of those who were far away, and denied the sad privilege of paying the last tender rites to the dead. Poor children! Poor mother! How my heart ached to think that mine must be the task to tell them the story of death, of which, perhaps, they were not dreaming now!

Before I had finished a boy came in hurriedly and said something to the steward, of which I caught only the words, "been fighting all day ... rebels attacked them this morning ... had a very hard time of it."

I grew for a moment sick with a terrible fear. A battle had taken place, and who should say how many lives in a few short hours had been crowned with the thorny wreath of affliction? It might be that I, too, was destined to feel the force of an awful blow. If so, God help me!

I could gain no particulars at the hospital, and was forced to wait until I reached home. There I learned that an attack had been made upon our forces Sunday morning, and the Confederates had occupied our camps for some time. Afterward they were driven out again, but we had lost many lives. They were still fighting an hour before nightfall. Further than this nothing was known.

All night I walked the floor in an agony of suspense and dread. Would the morning's dawn come to me with a message of gladness; or should I rank among the doomed, who henceforth must walk the earth in the darkness and gloom of utter desolation?

Ah, how I prayed that night! How I wrestled with my own fearful heart, and chided myself for the lack of faith which should have borne me up in that hour!

Monday came, freighted with death to thousands! All day the battle raged, and at night it was said that the Federals had achieved a great victory. A victory it was; but oh! at what a fearful cost! How many hundreds of young heads were that day laid low in the dust, never to rise again! How many hopeful hearts throbbed their last impulses of human aspirations and ambition!

Tuesday and Wednesday brought hundreds from the field of action. Some of the wounded were transported to Paducah, and I was called upon to dress their wounds and to assist in amputations, which required all the strength I possessed. The duty was a terrible one; but I nerved myself resolutely to perform it, hoping that, if need be, some one would as willingly attend to one of whose fate I had as yet learned nothing.

On Thursday morning the St. Francis Hotel was alive with officers from Shiloh, but still I was left in ignorance of my husband's fate, and the suspense was becoming insupportable. Every excuse that could be made for a delay of tidings had been utterly exhausted, and I felt now that he was either killed or wounded.

In the hope of hearing something definite I went out to the table for the first time since the battle, and took by usual seat, near which sat two wounded officers. One had his head bandaged; the other's arm was in a sling; and both were pale and weary-looking. But they were talking of the late contest, and after listening for a few moments I yielded to an uncontrollable impulse and asked the one nearest me if he knew any thing of the fate of the——Regiment.

He turned politely, with a look of interest I could but remark, and answered:

"I am sorry to say, madam, that it fared very badly. Some other regiments of the same division showed the white feather, and perfectly panic-stricken, broke ranks and fled. That gallant regiment alone stood its ground, and was literally cut to pieces. Those who were not killed were taken prisoners, only a few escaping."

"And the officers—were they all—?" I could not finish the sentence for the deathly sickness that was choking my utterance, and he answered it gently:

"I believe every one was killed. Did you have any friends among them, may I ask?"

"My husband," I gasped. "Captain S——."

I saw them exchange glances; and then, as if in a dream, a voice seemed to murmur afar off amidst the rushing of waters.

"Poor thing! He fell in the first onset. But see! She is falling!"

A strong hand grasped my arm, and a glass of water was pressed to my lips; but the shock of that deadly blow was too heavy, and I sank slowly into utter oblivion, conscious of a wish, as sight and sound faded, that I might never waken again!

It was an hour before they brought me back to a sense of my bereavement, and then I turned from the kind faces clustered about the couch to which I had been borne, and gave vent to a bitter cry.

"Ah? why did you not let me die? The world is so cold and desolate!"

Two firm, soft hands clasped mine, and drew them away from my face, and I saw the mild, reproachful eyes of a stranger gazing into mine. He was an old man, with hair as white as the snows of winter, and a voice soft and gentle as a tender mother's.

"My child, you are rebellious! Rouse yourself, and learn to say, Not my will, but thine, O Lord, be done!"

"I can not!—I can not bring myself to feel that there is any mercy or love in the power that could deal such a blow. God knew that he was all I had on earth, and he has taken him from me. It was cruel!"

"Hush! Resignation will come when you have time to think. Perhaps, after all, it is a mistake. There has been no official report of your husband's death, and he may only be wounded or a prisoner."

I started up, wild with the hope his words awakened.

"Nay, be not too hasty! I only say it may be possible."

I was silenced, but the hope was not crushed. It stung me to life again, and made every idle moment seem like an eternity of agony.

In a few moments they began to leave the room, and only one or two ladies remained in conversation with the old gentleman, who was a physician, and had been summoned hastily when I fainted. Seeing them thus engaged, I formed a sudden resolution, and raised myself from the pillows.

"What are you going to do?" asked the doctor, turning his face toward me.

"Find my husband—dead or alive," I answered, getting off the bed.

"My dear child, you are mad!" he expostulated. "You can not do any thing. Look at your face—it is as pallid as marble, and your eyes would frighten any one."

"That is because I have not slept or eaten scarcely since last Saturday night," I said, in reply. "Besides, I have been half mad with suspense. Only for the sick at the hospital, who claimed my care, I don't think I could have borne it at all."

"Go back and lie down on the bed," pleaded one of the ladies. "It makes my heart ache to look at you."

"How dreadfully you must have suffered!"

"God and my own heart only know how much," I answered, gulping down a sob. Her tone of womanly sympathy shook my strong self-control till I trembled. Than I broke down entirely, and with a bitter cry fell upon my knees by a chair.

"O Charley, Charley! my heart is breaking!"

Instantly her kind arms were twined round me—her soft lips pressed to my forehead. She held me to her heart, and suffered me to weep until the fountain of my tears was exhausted.

"There! you feel better now, don't you?" said the doctor, kindly. "You must lie down and keep quiet a while, or you will be ill. Your hands are like two burning coals now, while only a moment since they were like ice. You must not fall ill."

"Oh no! I can not afford to be ill. I must search for my husband," I answered, rising. "There—it is over now! I am done with tears for the present, and am ready to work. If I do not, I shall soon lose my reason. Don't talk to me, any of you!" I cried, as I saw them about to remonstrate. "I am determined to go up the river, and if I should never return, try to remember me kindly."

"The authorities will not permit you to go," said the doctor. "An order has been issued to allow no lady to pass up the river, and Colonel N—— has locked himself up to escape the importunities of the people."

"I shall go, nevertheless," was my reply.

"How will you manage it?" asked the old man, curiously.

"I don't know yet. But I shall go. Before night I will be on my way to Pittsburg Landing."

They looked at me pityingly; but I paid no attention further, and when they left the room I began to pack some articles in a small trunk which I could easily take with me.

About noon a boat, chartered at Cincinnati and sent after the wounded, touched at Paducah, and I obtained passage. Fortune seemed to favor me here, for I not only found myself able to carry out my design, but came into the midst of sympathizing friends, who received me cordially, and did all in their power to make me comfortable.

There were a number of surgeons and their assistants on board. Three Sisters of Charity and two ladies from Cincinnati completed the list, and in about an hour we entered the mouth of the river and proceeded on our sorrowful errand.

I will not dwell upon the tediousness of the trip. To me it seemed like an eternity of misery. On Thursday, about one o'clock, we left Paducah, and did not arrive at Pittsburg Landing until Saturday night, near eight o'clock.

I shall never forget that night or a single incident connected with it. As we made fast to the shore I was standing upon the hurricane deck, looking abroad, with my heart full of a wild and bitter fear. Here was Shiloh! There were the black, forbidding bluffs directly over my head, the banks of the river lined with boats from which profane and noisy men were unloading Government stores. Across the river two or three gunboats stretched their black, snake-like lengths along the waters, and from them only a fiery gleam was now and then discernible. Above, the sky was clear and blue, and studded with myriads of stars that looked, oh so calmly! down upon the terrible spot. There, where rivers of blood had flowed, lay the silvery white moonbeams, and on the death-laden air floated the rich perfume of spring flowers.

Even while I stood looking around me the *Continental* swung loose from her fastenings, and rounded out into the stream followed by half a dozen others. Now the lights blazed from every vessel, and a band struck up "Dixie" in the most spirited manner.

General Halleck was going up the river to destroy a bridge, and, convoyed by two of the gunboats, they started two and two abreast, keeping in this order until a sudden turn hid them from sight.

Turning my face once more toward the shore, some dark objects became visible lying some distance up the side of the hill; but I could not discern precisely what they were, and the next moment my attention was absorbed in a painful scene taking place on the deck of a boat just along side of the *Lancaster*.

There were a number of men lying upon berths in the open air, and around one of them was a surgeon and his group of assistants. The wounded man had his arm bared to the shoulder, and had I not seen the glittering of instruments in the light of the numerous lamps held around him I should still have divined his fate. Poor fellow! I heard him sob and plead piteously, "Oh, doctor, don't take my arm off! If I lose it my little sister will have no one to work for her. I'd rather die!"

"Die you will if it does not come off, and that very soon," was the response. "No help for it, boy, so be a man and bear it bravely."

The next moment a handkerchief was held to his face, and after a brief struggle he yielded to the powerful influence of chloroform. I hear the deep, quick gasping so painful to the listener and the tears ran down my cheeks unrestrainedly.

Captain V—— came up to me.

"Mrs. S——, I have been making inquiries for you, and can gain no intelligence whatever concerning your husband. I see no way but to wait until daylight and then I will find a conveyance and send some one with you."

"Can not I go tonight? It seems as if it is impossible to wait."

"No, it is out of the question. The mud is two feet deep on shore, and it is quite dark in the woods. I am sorry for you, but it will be only a little while longer. Try to be as patient as you can."

"Thank you, I will. But it is very, very hard."

"I am sure of it. But let me say a word to you here, Mrs. S——. I fear you are hoping too much. Remember he fell early on Sunday, and the chances are that he was hastily buried with many other in the trenches."

"For Heaven's sake go no further!" I implored. "My husband buried in a trench! Oh, God forbid!"

He took my hand, and drawing it within his arm led me to the ladies' cabin, which now presented a singular appearance, converted as it was into a hospital, and peopled by the wounded which the men were carrying on board.

There were three rows of mattresses spread upon the floor, the one in the middle capable of accommodating two patients, and one on each side a single man.

All these were filled already, and the clamor was terrible. Some called for food, others for water, and a few lay moaning piteously, their hunger and thirst forgotten in the sharp pain of undressed wounds.

One boy near the stern of the boat seemed to be in such distress that I hastened to his side and bent over him.

"Where are you wounded?" I asked.

"In the shoulder. I got it Monday, and it's never been dressed. I can not get at it myself."

Hastily getting a basin of water, sponge, and bandages, I exposed the inflamed and swollen shoulder and began to bathe it carefully. He regarded me for a moment with wide, fearful eyes, then as he felt the gentle touch and cooling sponge, his eyes closed and he heaved a great sigh of relief.

"Ah, that is so nice!" he murmured, presently. "I tell you it's hard enough to be shot down like a dog; but when it comes to lying out for a whole week in the open air, with only a blanket, a cracker, and a slice of dried beef, with an occasional drink of water, it's harder still. I thought I should starve to death before they could get a boat to take us off, and if I could only have had my shoulder dressed! Oh, how good that feels!"

I had just laid a folded napkin wet with ice water over the wound, and it was this which called forth such an exclamation of delight.

"I am glad you feel better. Now I am going to bring you a cup of tea, with some bread and butter. If you are so nearly starved, it is time you should have something to eat."

"Oh, thank you!"

I hastened away, and in a few moments came back with the tea and bread, which he ate like a man who was indeed starving. The glare of his large dark eyes was perfectly terrible.

"More, more!" he gasped pantingly, swallowing the last drop of tea at a draught.

"Not now. In half an hour you shall have more. To give it you now will do you more harm than good. We must try to keep down fever. Now, shall I bathe you face and hands for you?"

"If you please," with an eager, wistful look at the empty cup and plate that made my eyes grow humid.

While I was engaged in the operation Doctor P——, from Cincinnati, passed me.

"Who taught you to nurse?" he asked. "I wish all women would take right hold of the boys as you do. There would be less suffering."

"They have surely earned this much at our hands, at least," I said, in reply.

"Ay, to be sure. But I know plenty who would never get down on their knees on the floor as you are doing, and take hold of an object like that."

"I hope not. I believe there are few who would not do it if in such circumstances. There is not one who has a father, brother, or husband in the service who would refuse to do it, I am sure."

He passed on with some careless reply, and I continued attending the soldiers until it grew late. After three o'clock I threw myself upon a sofa in the chamber-maid's room, and slept until half past five. Then I rose and went again among the wounded until such an hour as I could set out upon my journey over the field.

I will here mention a case that may seem incredible to many; but if so, it will not surprise me, for I could scarcely believe the evidence of my own senses, when one of the surgeons came to me directly after I entered the cabin the night before, and asked me to come and "see a sight." I told him I would as soon as I finished "feeding my patient;" and did so, he meeting me half-way when he saw me coming.

About midway of the cabin lay a rebel prisoner, badly wounded in the head. A ball had passed behind his eyes, forcing both upon the cheeks, where they lay in a most horrible and swollen condition. From the wounds in each temple a portion of the brain was slowly oozing, and the doctor pointed to it, saying,

"In all my life I have seen nothing like that. He has been lying here for the last ten minutes in that condition, quarreling with the Federal soldier just opposite."

"Surely he can not know what he is saying!" I ejaculated.

"Yes, he does, perfectly. You should hear him."

I had an opportunity soon, for in a moment he called out:

"Say! look here, Yank! I want a drink of water!"

"All right! You shall have it in a moment," answered one of the men in waiting. "I'm tending to a feller, and shall be done in a minute."

"Oh, yes, I'll be bound you'll tend to your Yanks before you do to me! But when a man's on his last legs you might stop a moment to give him a drop of water. I sha'n't ask it of you more than an hour or so longer. Then I'm going straight to ——!"

I shuddered and retreated from the spot. Such profanity and recklessness upon the very brink of eternity! It was awful!

"Poor wretch! Good pity and have mercy upon you!" said the doctor. "You have none for yourself."

"I don't want any of your cant, Sir," said the man, in reply. "My soul is not yours, and you need not trouble yourself about it in the least."

When I came again into the cabin the following morning he was just breathing his last—going home to his Creator hardened, reckless—utterly careless of the fate that awaited him.

An hour later Captain V—— sent for a conveyance, but could get none, to carry me over the field in search of the camp from which I hoped to gain some intelligence that should end suspense. While striving to devise some means the medical director of the —— Division came on board, and offered me one of his horses, proposing himself to guide me to the place where the —— Regiment was camped. There were but few left, he said, but what there were had pitched their tents about five miles distant, and he thought he could take me to the place without difficulty.

Thanking him warmly I accepted the offer, and erelong found myself mounted and laboring through the mud up the side of the bluff.

The path led round it, ascending gradually to the top, and once upon the shore, I discovered the dark objects that had puzzled me the night previous were human bodies lying under the broiling sun waiting for burial.

Through the mud, over fallen trees, broken artillery, and pieces of shells, the carcasses of horses and mules, and by strips of woodland cut down like grass by the rains of iron and lead! How strange and solemn and fearful it seemed! Giant trees pierced by balls and shorn of their bark till the trunks showed a hundred grinning scars; boughs severed and hanging by a single fibre, or lying prone upon the ground, trampled and blood-stained!

Our progress was slow. It was long past noon when we reached the little hollow in which the tents I sought had been pitched; and then, as we came in sight of the little blue wreaths of smoke, and saw a few solitary men moving about, I began to tremble. I knew that I was about to meet my fate, and the thought of what it might be almost deprived me of the necessary strength to go on to the end.

Presently, after passing through several encampments, we descended into the hollow and alighted before the officers' quarters, which seemed almost deserted. There the doctor bade me go in and wait while he made inquires of those around outside.

On first entering I saw nothing but a berth, on which lay a man with has face turned from me; but the next moment I discovered that another was seated beyond, his head resting against the side of the berth, fast asleep. A pillow supported the right arm of the invalid, and by the bandages I knew he had been wounded. My heart swelled with pity, and stealing softly toward the bed, I leaned over to catch a glimpse of his face.

Pale—oh, so pale and wan! with the rich brown hair pushed back from the broad brow, pure and white as marble. The blue eyes were half closed, and the lips parted with such an expression of suffering that a loving woman's heart might almost break in looking upon it. Yet I did not moan, nor faint, nor cry out. I only fell upon my knees, and taking the white, clammy fingers of the left hand in my own, covered it with warm tears and gentle kisses—for it was my own dear husband, whom God had spared to me, and I had found him at last!

"I thank Thee, O my Father!" was the cry of my soul in that hour, and my lips breathed it audibly. With the sound Charley opened his eyes and looked into my face with a bewildered stare. Then a light broke all over his pale face, and his glad smile sent happy tears raining over my cheeks.

"Is it you, darling? I thought you would never come!" he breathed faintly. "But you are here now, and you will not leave me again, will you?"

"No, indeed. I will take care of you, and get you well again. Ah, how you must have missed me!"

"Missed you! It has been an eternity of misery since I fell, and I have called your name vainly a thousand times."

"They told me you were killed!" I said, chokingly. "I waited for tidings from you till I thought I should go mad, and then they said you were dead, and when I declared my intention of finding you, tried to keep me from coming. But I would not be stayed, and, thank God! I have found you alive."

"Ay! Thank God from your soul, for it is one of His greatest blessings that he is here now!" said the doctor, who had entered and laid his hand upon my head.

"Tell her all about it," whispered by husband's faint voice, and as his fingers clasped mine closer the old man sat down upon a campstool and began:

"I have just heard the story from one of the boys, and it is a wonder to me how he lived through that long time without the least care. He must have crept into the thicket where they found him very soon after falling, and there remained for four days. There was a dead soldier near him, and from his canteen and haversack he managed to obtain water and food; but his wound bled terribly. They say, to judge by the stains around and where they came across him, he had just a spark of life left. He will need you now to nurse him back to life again, and it will take nice nursing too."

"Will he lose his arm, doctor?" I asked, in a suppressed voice, lest

Charley should hear.

"I will tell you after a while," was the answer; and accordingly "after a while" he examined it closely. As he left the tent I followed him out.

"Well, doctor?"

"All right, my little anxious woman! The Captain can carry that arm through several campaigns yet, I hope," he said, heartily; and I went back to my boy, my eyes wet with glad tears.

Three weeks later we were within our own quiet home, where I was nursing him back to strength to be ready for the Fall campaign.

Mary Bowman

Elsie Singmaster

Outside the broad gateway which leads into the National Cemetery at Gettysburg and thence on into the great park, there stands a little house on whose porch there may be seen on summer evenings an old woman. The cemetery with its tall monuments lies a little back of her and to her left; before her is the village; beyond, on a little eminence, the buildings of the Theological Seminary; and still farther beyond the foothills of the Blue Ridge. The village is tree-shaded, the hills are set with fine oaks and hickories, the fields are green. It would be difficult to find in all the world an expanse more lovely. Those who have known it in their youth grow homesick for it; their eyes ache and their throats tighten as they remember it. At sunset it is bathed in purple light, its trees grow darker, its hills more shadowy, its hollows deeper and more mysterious. Then, lifted above the dark masses of the trees, one may see marble shafts and domes turn to liquid gold.

The little old woman, sitting with folded hands, is Mary Bowman, whose husband was lost on this field. The battle will soon be fifty years in the past, she has been for that long a widow. She has brought up three children, two sons and a daughter. One of her sons is a merchant, one is a clergyman, and her daughter is well and happily married. Her own life of activity is past; she is waited upon tenderly and loved dearly by her children and her grandchildren. She was born in this village, she has almost never been away. From here her husband went to war, here he is buried among thousands of unknown dead, here she nursed the wounded and dying, here she will be buried herself in the Evergreen cemetery, beyond the National cemetery.

She has seen beauty change to desolation, trees shattered, fields trampled, walls broken, all her dear, familiar world turned to chaos; she has seen desolation grow again to beauty. These hills and streams were always lovely, now a nation has determined to keep them forever in the same loveliness. Here was a rocky, wooded field, destined by its owner to cultivation; it has been decreed that its rough picturesqueness shall endure forever. Here is a lowly farmhouse; upon it no hand of change shall be laid while the nation continues. Preserved, consecrated, hallowed are the woods and lanes in which Mary Bowman walked with the lover of her youth.

Broad avenues lead across the fields, marking the lines where by thousands Northerners and Southerners were killed. Big Round Top, to which one used to journey by a difficult path, is now accessible; Union and Confederate soldiers, returning, find their way with ease to old positions; lads from West Point are brought to see, spread out before them as on a map, that Union fish-hook, five miles long, inclosing that slightly curved Confederate line.

Monuments are here by hundreds, names by thousands, cast in bronze, as endurable as they can be made by man. All that can be done in remembrance of those who fought here has been done, all possible effort to identify the unknown has been made. For fifty years their little trinkets have been preserved, their pocket Testaments, their photographs, their letters — letters addressed to "My precious son," "My dear brother," "My beloved husband." Seeing them today, you will find them marked by a number. This stained scapular, this little housewife with its rusty scissors, this unsigned letter, dated in '63, belonged to him who lies now in Grave Number 20 or Number 3500.

There is almost an excess of tenderness for these dead, yet mixed with it is a strange feeling of remoteness. We mourn them, praise them, laud them, but we cannot understand them. To this generation war is strange, its sacrifices are uncomprehended, incomprehensible. It is especially so in these latter years, since those who came once to this field come now no more. Once the heroes of the war were familiar figures upon these streets; Meade with his serious, bearded face, Slocum with his quick, glancing eyes, Hancock with his distinguished air, Howard with his empty sleeve. They have gone hence, and with them have marched two thirds of Gettysburg's two hundred thousand.

Mary Bowman has seen them all, has heard them speak. Sitting on her little porch, she has watched most of the great men of the United States go by, Presidents, cabinet officials, ambassadors, army officers, and also famous visitors from other lands who know little of the United States, but to whom Gettysburg is as a familiar country. She has watched also that great, rapidly shrinking army of private soldiers in faded blue coats, who make pilgrimages to see the fields and hills upon which they fought. She has tried to make herself realize that her husband, if he had lived, would be like these old men, maimed, feeble, decrepit, but the thought possesses no reality for her. He is still young, still erect, he still goes forth in the pride of life and strength.

Mary Bowman will not talk about the battle. To each of her children and each of her grandchildren, she has told once, as one who performs a sacred duty, its many-sided story. She has told each one of wounds and suffering, but she has not omitted tales of heroic death, of promotion on the field, of stubborn fight for glory. By others than her own she will not be questioned. A young officer, recounting the rigors of the march, has written, "Forsan et haec olim meminisse juvabit," — "Perchance even these things it will be delightful to remember." To feel delight, remembering these things, Mary Bowman has never learned. Her neighbors who suffered with her, some just as cruelly, have recovered; their wounds have healed, as wounds do in the natural course of things. But Mary Bowman has remained mindful; she has been, for all these years, widowed indeed.

Her faithful friend and neighbor, Hannah Casey, is the great joy of visitors to the battlefield. She will talk incessantly, enthusiastically, with insane invention. The most morbid visitor will be satisfied with Hannah's wild account of a Valley of Death filled to the rim with dead bodies, of the trickling rivulet of Plum Creek swollen with blood to a roaring torrent. But Mary Bowman is different.

Her granddaughter, who lives with her, is curious about her emotions. "Do you feel reconciled?" she will ask. "Do you feel reconciled to the sacrifice, grandmother? Do you think of the North and South as reunited, and are you glad you helped?"

Her grandmother answers with no words, but with a slow, tearful smile. She does not analyze her emotions. Perhaps it is too much to expect of one who has been a widow for fifty years, that she philosophize about it!

Sitting on her porch in the early morning, she remembers the first of July, fifty years ago.

"Madam!" cried the soldier who galloped to the door, "there is to be a battle in this town!"

"Here?" she had answered stupidly. *"Here?"*

Sitting there at noon, she hears the roaring blasts of artillery, she seems to see shells, as of old, curving like great ropes through the air, she remembers that somewhere on this field, struck by a missile such as that, her husband fell.

Sitting there in the moonlight, she remembers Early on his white horse, with muffled hoofs, riding spectralwise down the street among the sleeping soldiers.

"Up, boys!" he whispers, and is heard even in that heavy stupor. "Up, boys, up! We must get away!"

She hears also the pouring rain of July the fourth, falling upon her little house, upon that wide battle-field, upon her very heart. She sees, too, the deep, sad eyes of Abraham Lincoln, she hears his voice in the great sentences of his simple speech, she feels his message in her soul.

"Daughter!" he seems to say, "Daughter, be of good comfort!"

So, still, Mary Bowman sits waiting. She is a Christian, she has great hope; as her waiting has been long, so may the joy of her reunion be full.

The Blue and the Grey
A HOSPITAL SKETCH

Louisa May Alcott

D on't bring him in here; every corner is full—and I'm glad of it," added the nurse under her breath, eyeing with strong disfavor the gaunt figure lying on the stretcher in the doorway.

"Where shall we put him, then? They won't have him in either of the other wards on this floor. He's ordered up here, and here he must stay if he's put in the hall—poor devil!" said the foremost bearer, looking around the crowded room in despair.

The nurse's eye followed his, and both saw a thin hand beckoning from the end of the long ward.

"It's Murry; I'll see what he wants;" and Miss Mercy went to him with her quick, noiseless step, and the smile her grave face always wore for him.

"There's room here, if you turn my bed 'round, you see. Don't let them leave him in the hall," said Murry, lifting his great eyes to hers. Brilliant with the fever burning his strength away, and pathetic with the silent protest of life against death.

"It's like you to think of it; but he's a rebel," began Miss Mercy.

"So much more reason to take him in. I don't mind having him here;

but it will distress me dreadfully to know that any poor soul was turned away, from the comfort of this ward especially."

The look he gave her made the words an eloquent compliment, and his pity for a fallen enemy reproached her for her own lack of it. Her face softened as she nodded, and glanced about the recess.

"You will have the light in your eyes, and only the little table between you and a very disagreeable neighbor," she said.

"I can shut my eyes if the light troubles them; I've nothing else to do now," he answered, with a faint laugh. "I was too comfortable before; I'd more than my share of luxuries; so bring him along, and it will be all right."

The order was given, and, after a brief bustle, the two narrow beds stood side by side in the recess under the organ-loft—for the hospital had been a church. Left alone for a moment, the two men eyed each other silently. Murry saw a tall, sallow man, with fierce black eyes, wild hair and beard, and a thin-lipped, cruel mouth. A ragged gray uniform was visible under the blanket thrown over him; and in strange contrast to the squalor of his dress, and the neglect of his person, was the diamond ring that shone on his unwounded hand. The right arm was bound up, the right leg amputated at the knee; and though the man's face was white and haggard with suffering, not a sound escaped him as he lay with his bold eyes fixed defiantly upon his neighbor.

John Clay, the new-comer, saw opposite him a small, wasted figure, and a plain face; yet both face and figure were singularly attractive, for suffering seemed to have refined away all the grosser elements, and left the spiritual very visible through that frail tenement of flesh. Pale-brown hair streaked the hollow temples and white forehead. A deep color burned in the thin cheeks still tanned by the wind and weather of a long campaign. The mouth was grave and sweet, and in the gray eyes lay an infinite patience touched with melancholy. He wore a dressing-gown, but across his feet lay a faded coat of army-blue. As the other watched him, he saw a shadow pass across his tranquil face, and for a moment he laid his wasted hand over the eyes that had been so full of pity. Then he gently pushed a mug of fresh water, and the last of a bunch of grapes, toward the exhausted rebel, saying, in a cordial tone, "You look faint and thirsty; have 'em."

Clay's lips were parched, and his hand went involuntarily toward the cup; but he caught it back, and leaning forward, asked in a shrill whisper,

"Where are you hurt?"

"A shot in the side," answered Murry, visibly surprised at the man's manner.

"What battle?"

"The Wilderness."

"Is it bad?"

"I'm dying of wound-fever; there's no hope, they say."

That reply, so simple, so serenely given, would have touched almost any hearer; but Clay smiled grimly, and lay down as if satisfied, with his one hand clenched, and an exulting glitter in his eyes, muttering to himself,

"The loss of my leg comes easier after hearing that."

Murry saw his lips move, but caught no sound, and asked with friendly solicitude,

"Do you want any thing, neighbor?"

"Yes—to be let alone," was the curt reply, with a savage frown.

"That's easily done. I sha'n't trouble you very long, any way;" and, with a sigh, Murry turned his face away, and lay silent till the surgeon came up on his morning round.

"Oh, you're here, are you? It's like Mercy Carrol to take you in," said Dr. Fitz Hugh as he surveyed the rebel with a slight frown; for, in spite of his benevolence and skill, he was a stanch loyalist, and hated the South as he did sin.

"Don't praise me; he never would have been here but for Murry," answered Miss Mercy, as she approached with her dressing-tray in her hand.

"Bless the lad! he'll give up his bed next, and feel offended if he's thanked for it. How are you, my good fellow?" and the doctor turned to press the hot hand with a friendly face.

"Much easier and stronger, thank you, doctor," was the cheerful answer.

"Less fever, pulse better, breath freer—good symptoms. Keep on so for twenty-four hours, and by my soul, I believe you'll have a chance for your life, Murry," cried the doctor, as his experienced eye took note of a hopeful change.

"In spite of the opinion of three good surgeons to the contrary?" asked Murry, with a wistful smile.

"Hang every body's opinion! We are but mortal men, and the best of us make mistakes in spite of science and experience. There's Parker; we all gave him up, and the rascal is larking 'round Washington as well as ever to-day. While there's life, there's hope; so cheer up, my lad, and do your best for the little girl at home."

"Do you really think I may hope?" cried Murry, white with the joy of this unexpected reprieve.

"Hope is a capital medicine, and I prescribe it for a day at least. Don't build on this change too much, but if you are as well to-morrow as this morning, I give you my word I think you'll pull through."

Murry laid his hands over his face with a broken "Thank God for that!" and the doctor turned away with a sonorous "Hem!" and an air of intense satisfaction.

During this conversation Miss Mercy had been watching the rebel, who looked and listened to the others so intently that he forgot her presence. She saw an expression of rage and disappointment gather in his face as the doctor spoke; and when Murry accepted the hope held out to him, Clay set his teeth with an evil look, that would have boded ill for his neighbor had he not been helpless.

"Ungrateful traitor! I'll watch him, for he'll do mischief if he can," she thought, and reluctantly began to unbind his arm for the doctor's inspection.

"Only a flesh-wound—no bones broken—a good syringing, rubber cushion, plenty of water, and it will soon heal. You'll attend to that Miss Mercy; this stump is more in my line;" and Dr. Fitz Hugh turned to the leg, leaving the arm to the nurse's skilful care.

"Evidently amputated in a hurry, and neglected since. If you're not careful, young man, you'll change places with your neighbor here."

"Damn him!" muttered Clay in his beard, with an emphasis which caused the doctor to glance at his vengeful face.

"Don't be a brute, if you can help it. But for him, you'd have fared ill," began the doctor.

"But for him, I never should have been here," muttered the man in French, with a furtive glance about the room.

"You owe this to him?" asked the doctor, touching the wound, and speaking in the same tongue.

"Yes; but he paid for it—at least, I thought he had."

"By the Lord! if you are the sneaking rascal that shot him as he lay wounded in the ambulance, I shall be tempted to leave you to your fate!" cried the doctor, with a wrathful flash in his keen eyes.

"Do it, then, for it was I," answered the man defiantly; adding as if anxious to explain, "We had a tussle, and each got hurt in the thick of the skirmish. He was put in the ambulance afterward, and I was left to live or die, as luck would have it. I was hurt the worst; they should have taken me too; it made me mad to see him chosen, and I fired my last shot as he drove away. I didn't know whether I hit him or not; but when they told me I must lose my leg, I hoped I had, and now I am satisfied."

He spoke rapidly, with clenched hand and fiery eyes, and the two listeners watched him with a sort of fascination as he hissed out the last words, glancing at the occupant of the next bed. Murry evidently did not understand French; he lay with averted face, closed eyes, and a hopeful smile still on his lips, quite unconscious of the meaning of the fierce words uttered close beside him. Dr. Fitz Hugh had laid down his instruments and knit his black brows irefully while he listened. But as the man paused, the doctor looked at Miss Mercy, who was quietly going on with her work, though there was an expression about her handsome mouth that made her womanly face look almost grim. Taking up his tools, the doctor followed her example, saying slowly,

"If I didn't believe Murry was mending, I'd turn you over to Roberts, whom the patients dread as they do the devil. I must do my duty, and you may thank Murry for it."

"Does he know you are the man who shot him?" asked Mercy, still in French.

"No; I shouldn't stay here long if he did," answered Clay, with a short laugh.

"Don't tell him, then—at least, till after you are moved," she said, in a tone of command.

"Where am I going?" demanded the man.

"Anywhere out of my ward," was the brief answer, with a look that made the black eyes waver and fall.

In silence nurse and doctor did their work, and passed on. In silence Murry lay hour after hour, and silently did Clay watch and wait, till, utterly exhausted by the suffering he was too proud to confess, he sank into a stupor, oblivious alike of hatred, defeat, and pain. Finding him in this pitiable condition, Mercy relented, and woman-like, forgot her contempt in pity. He was not moved, but tended carefully all that day and night; and when he woke from a heavy sleep, the morning sun shone again on two pale faces in the beds, and flashed on the buttons of two army-coats hanging side by side on the recess wall, on loyalist and rebel, on the blue and the gray.

Dr. Fitz Hugh stood beside Murry's cot, saying cheerily, "You are doing well, my lad—better than I hoped. Keep calm and cool, and, if all goes right, we'll have little Mary here to pet you in a week."

"Who's Mary?" whispered the rebel to the attendant who was washing his face.

"His sweetheart; he left her for the war, and she's waitin' for him back—poor soul!" answered the man, with a somewhat vicious scrub across the sallow cheek he was wiping.

"So he'll get well, and go home and marry the girl he left behind him, will he?" sneered Clay, fingering a little case that hung around his neck, and was now visible as his rough valet unbuttoned his collar.

"What's that—your sweetheart's picter?" asked Ben, the attendant, eyeing the gold chain anxiously.

"I've got none," was the gruff answer.

"So much the wus for you, then. Small chance of gettin' one here; our girls won't look at you, and you a'n't likely to see any of your own sort for a long spell, I reckon," added Ben, rasping away at the rebel's long-neglected hair.

Clay lay looking at Mercy Carrol as she went to and fro among the men, leaving a smile behind her, and carrying comfort wherever she turned,—a right womanly woman, lovely and lovable, strong yet tender, patient yet decided, skilful, kind, and tireless in the discharge of duties that would have daunted most women. It was in vain she wore the plain gray gown and long apron, for neither could hide the grace of her figure. It was in vain she brushed her luxuriant hair back in a net, for the wavy locks would fall on her forehead, and stray curls would creep out or glisten like gold under the meshes meant to conceal them. Busy days and watchful nights had not faded the beautiful bloom on her cheeks, or dimmed the brightness of her hazel eyes. Always ready, fresh, and fair, Mercy Carrol was regarded as the good angel of the hospital, and not a man in it, sick or well, but was a loyal friend to her. None dared to be a lover, for her little romance was known; and, though still a maid, she was a widow in their eyes, for she had sent her lover to his death, and over the brave man's grave had said, "Well done."

Ben watched Clay as his eye followed the one female figure there, and, observing that he clutched the case still tighter, asked again,

"What is that—a charm?"

"Yes—against pain, captivity , and shame."

"Strikes me it a'n't kep' you from any one of 'em," said Ben, with a laugh.

"I haven't tried it yet."

"How does it work?" Ben asked more respectfully, being impressed by something in the rebel's manner.

"You will see when I use it. Now let me alone," and Clay turned impatiently away.

"You've got p'ison, or some deviltry, in that thing. If you don't let me look, I swear I'll have it took away from you; and Ben put his big hand on the slender chain with a resolute air.

Clay smiled a scornful smile, and offered the trinket, saying coolly,

"I only fooled you. Look as much as you like; you'll find nothing dangerous."

Ben opened the pocket, saw a curl of gray hair, and nothing more.

"Is that your mother's?"

"Yes; my dead mother's."

It was strange to see the instantaneous change that passed over the two men as each uttered that dearest word in all tongues. Rough Ben gently reclosed and returned the case, saying kindly, "Keep it; I wouldn't rob you on't for no money."

Clay thrust it jealously into his breast, and the first trace of emotion he had shown softened his dark face, as he answered, with a grateful tremor in his voice.

"Thank you. I wouldn't lose it for the world."

"May I say good morning, neighbor?" asked a feeble voice, as Murry turned a very wan but cheerful face toward him, when Ben moved on with his basin and towel.

"If you like," returned Clay, looking at him with those quick, suspicious eyes of his.

"Well, I do like; so I say it, and hope you are better," returned the cordial voice.

"Are you?"

"Yes, thank God!"

"Is it sure?"

"Nothing is sure, in a case like mine, till I'm on my legs again; but I'm certainly better. I don't expect you to be glad, but I hope you don't regret it very much."

"I don't." The smile that accompanied the words surprised Murry as much as the reply, for both seemed honest, and his kind heart warmed toward his suffering enemy.

"I hope you'll be exchanged as soon as you are able. Till then, you can go to one of the other hospitals, where there are many reb—I would say, Southerners. If you'd like, I'll speak to Dr. Fitz Hugh, and he'll see you moved," said Murry, in his friendly way.

"I'd rather stay here, thank you." Clay smiled again as he spoke in the mild tone that surprised Murry as much as it pleased him.

"You like to be in my corner, then?" he said, with a boyish laugh.

"Very much—for a while."

"I'm very glad. Do you suffer much?"

"I shall suffer more by and by, if I go on; but I'll risk it," answered Clay, fixing his feverish eyes on Murry's placid face.

"You expect to have a hard time with your leg?" said Murry, compassionately.

"With my soul."

It was an odd answer, and given with such an odd expression, as Clay turned his face away, that Murry said no more, fancying his brain a little touched by the fever evidently coming on.

They spoke but seldom to each other that day, for Clay lay apparently asleep, with a flushed cheek and restless head, and Murry tranquilly dreamed waking dreams of home and little Mary. That night, after all was still, Miss Mercy went up into the organ-loft to get fresh rollers for the morrow—the boxes of old linen, and such matters, being kept there. As she stood looking down on the thirty pale sleepers, she remembered that she had not played a hymn on the little organ for Murry, as she had promised that day. Stealing softly to the front, she peeped over the gallery, to see if he was asleep; if not, she would keep her word, for he was her favorite.

A screen had been drawn before the recess where the two beds stood, shutting their occupants from the sight of the other men. Murry lay sleeping, but Clay was awake, and a quick thrill tingled along the young woman's nerves as she saw his face. Leaning on one arm, he peered about the place with an eager, watchful air, and glanced up at the dark gallery, but did not see the startled face behind the central pillar. Pausing an instant, he shook his one clenched hand at the unconscious sleeper, and then drew out the locket cautiously. Two white mugs just alike stood on the little table between the beds, water in each. With another furtive glance about him, Clay suddenly stretched out his long arm, and dropped something from the locket into Murry's cup. An instant he remained motionless, with a sinister smile on his face; then, as Ben's step sounded beyond the screen, he threw his arm over his face, and lay, breathing heavily, as if asleep.

Mercy's first impulse was to cry out; her next, to fly down and seize the cup. No time was to be lost, for Murry might wake and drink at any moment. What was in the cup? Poison, doubtless; that was the charm Clay carried to free himself from "pain, captivity, and shame," when all other hopes of escape vanished. This hidden helper he gave up to destroy his enemy, who was to outlive his shot, it seemed. Like a shadow, Mercy glided down, forming her plan as she went. A dozen mugs stood about the room, all alike in size and color; catching up one, she partly filled it, and, concealing it under the clean sheet hanging on her arm, went toward the recess, saying audibly,

"I want some fresh water, Ben."

Thus warned of her approach, Clay lay with carefully-averted face as she came in, and never stirred as she bent over him, while she dexterously changed Murry's mug for the one she carried. Hiding the poisoned cup, she went away, saying aloud,

"Never mind the water, now, Ben. Murry is asleep, and so is Clay; they'll not need it yet."

Straight to Dr. Fitz Hugh's room she went, and gave the cup into his keeping, with the story of what she had seen. A man was dying, and there was no time to test the water then; but putting it carefully away, he promised to set her fears at rest in the morning. To quiet her impatience, Mercy went back to watch over Murry till day dawned. As she sat down, she caught a glimmer of a satisfied smile on Clay's lips, and looking into the cup she had left, she saw that it was empty.

"He is satisfied, for he thinks his horrible revenge is secure. Sleep in peace, my poor boy! you are safe while I am here."

As she thought this, she put her hand on the broad, pale forehead of the sleeper with a motherly caress, but started to feel how damp and cold it was. Looking nearer, she saw that a change had passed over Murry, for dark shadows showed about his sunken eyes, his once quiet breath was faint and fitful now, his hand deathly cold, and a chilly dampness had gathered on his face. She looked at her watch; it was past twelve, and her heart sunk within her, for she had so often seen that solemn change come over men's faces then, that the hour was doubly weird and woeful to her. Sending a message to Dr. Fitz Hugh, she waited anxiously, trying to believe that she deceived herself.

The doctor came at once, and a single look convinced him that he had left one death-bed for another.

"As I feared," he said; "that sudden rally was but a last effort of nature. There was just one chance for him, and he has missed it. Poor lad! I can do nothing; he'll sink rapidly, and go without pain."

"Can I do nothing?" asked Mercy, with dim eyes, as she held the cold hand close in both her own with tender pressure.

"Give him stimulants as long as he can swallow, and, if he's conscious, take any messages he may have. Poor Hall is dying hard, and I can help him; I'll come again in an hour and say good-by."

The kind doctor choked, touched the pale sleeper with a gentle caress, and went away to help Hall die.

Murry slept on for an hour, then woke, and knew without words that his brief hope was gone. He looked up wistfully, and whispered, as Mercy tried to smile with trembling lips that refused to tell the heavy truth.

"I know, I feel it; don't grieve yourself by trying to tell me, dear friend. It's best so; I can bear it, but I did want to live."

"Have you any word for Mary, dear?" asked Mercy, for he seemed but a boy to her since she had nursed him.

One look of sharp anguish and dark despair passed over his face, as he wrung his thin hands and shut his eyes, finding death terrible. It passed in a moment, and his pallid countenance grew beautiful with the pathetic patience of one who submits without complaint to the inevitable.

"Tell her I was ready, and the only bitterness was leaving her. I shall remember, and wait until she comes. My little Mary! oh, be kind to her, for my sake, when you tell her this."

"I will, Murry, as God hears me. I will be a sister to her while I live."

As Mercy spoke with fervent voice, he laid the hand that had ministered to him so faithfully against his cheek, and lay silent, as if content.

"What else? let me do something more. Is there no other friend to be comforted?"

"No; she is all I have in the world. I hoped to make her so happy, to be so much to her, for she's a lonely little thing; but God says 'No,' and I submit."

A long pause, as he lay breathing heavily, with eyes that were dimming fast fixed on the gentle face beside him.

"Give Ben my clothes; send Mary a bit of my hair, and—may I give you this? It's a poor thing, but all I have to leave you, best and kindest of women."

He tried to draw off a slender ring, but the strength had gone out of his wasted fingers, and she helped him, thanking him with the first tears he had seen her shed. He seemed satisfied, but suddenly turned his eyes on Clay, who lay as if asleep. A sigh broke from Murry, and Mercy caught the words,

"How could he do it, and I so helpless!"

"Do you know him?" she whispered, eagerly, as she remembered Clay's own words.

"I knew he was the man who shot me, when he came. I forgive him; but I wish he had spared me, for Mary's sake," he answered sorrowfully, not angrily.

"Can you really pardon him?" cried Mercy, wondering, yet touched by the words.

"I can. He will be sorry one day, perhaps; at any rate, he did what he thought his duty; and war makes brutes of us all sometimes, I fear. I'd like to say good-by; but he's asleep after a weary day, so don't wake him. Tell him I'm glad he is to live, and that I forgive him heartily."

Although uttered between long pauses, these words seemed to have exhausted Murry, and he spoke no more till Dr. Fitz Hugh came. To him he feebly returned thanks, and whispered his farewell—then sank into a stupor, during which life ebbed fast. Both nurse and doctor forgot Clay as they hung over Murry, and neither saw the strange intentness of his face, the half awe-struck, half remorseful look he bent upon the dying man.

As the sun rose, sending its ruddy beams across the silent ward, Murry looked up and smiled, for the bright ray fell athwart the two coats hanging on the wall beside him. Some passerby had brushed one sleeve of the blue coat across the gray, as if the inanimate things were shaking hands.

"It should be so—love our enemies; we should be brothers, " he murmured faintly; and, with the last impulse of a noble nature, stretched his hand toward the man who had murdered him.

But Clay shrunk back, and covered his face without a word. When he ventured to look up, Murry was no longer there. A pale, peaceful figure lay on the narrow bed, and Mercy was smoothing the brown locks as she cut a curl for Mary and herself. Clay could not take his eyes away; as if fascinated by its serenity, he watched the dead face with gloomy eyes, till Mercy, having done her part, stooped and kissed the cold lips tenderly as she left him to his sleep. Then, as if afraid to be alone with the dead, he bid Ben put the screen between the beds, and bring him a book. His order was obeyed, but he never turned his pages, and lay with muffled head trying to shut out little Watts' sobs, as the wounded drummer-boy mourned for Murry.

Death, in a hospital, makes no stir, and in an hour no trace of the departed remained but the coat upon the wall, for Ben would not take it down, though it was his now. The empty bed stood freshly made, the clean cup and worn Bible lay ready for other hands, and the card at the bed's head hung blank for a new-comer's name. In the hurry of this event, Clay's attempted crime was forgotten for a time. But that evening Dr. Fitz Hugh told Mercy that her suspicions were correct, for the water was poisoned.

"How horrible! What shall we do?" she cried, with a gesture full of energetic indignation.

"Leave him to remorse," replied the doctor, sternly. "I've thought over the matter, and believe this to be the only thing we can do. I fancy the man won't live a week; his leg is in a bad way, and he is such a fiery devil, he gives himself no chance. Let him believe he killed poor Murry, at least for a few days. He thinks so now, and tries to rejoice; but if he has a human heart, he will repent."

"But he may not. Should we not tell of this? Can he not be punished?"

"Law won't hang a dying man, and I'll not denounce him. Let remorse punish him while he lives, and God judge him when he dies. Murry pardoned him; can we do less?"

Mercy's indignant face softened at the name, and for Murry's sake she yielded. Neither spoke of what they tried to think the act of a half-delirious man; and soon they could not refuse to pity him, for the doctor's prophecy proved true.

Clay was a haunted man, and remorse gnawed like a worm at his heart. Day and night he saw the pale hand outstretched to him; day and night he heard the faint voice murmuring kindly, regretfully, "I forgive him; but I wish he had spared me, for Mary's sake."

As the days passed, and his strength visibly declined, he began to suspect that he must soon follow Murry. No one told him; for, though both doctor and nurse did their duty faithfully, neither lingered long at his bedside, and not one of the men showed any interest in him. No new patient occupied the other bed, and he lay alone in the recess with his own gloomy thoughts.

"It will be all up with me in a few days, won't it?" he asked abruptly, as Ben made his toilet one morning with unusual care, and such visible pity in his rough face that Clay could not but observe it.

"I heard the doctor say you wouldn't suffer much more. Is there any one you'd like to see, or leave a message for?" answered Ben, smoothing the long locks as gently as a woman.

"There isn't a soul in the world that cares whether I live or die, except the man who wants my money," said Clay, bitterly, as his dark face grew a shade paler at this confirmation of his fear.

"Can't you head him off some way, and leave your money to some one that's been kind to you? Here's the doctor—or, better still, Miss Carrol. Neither on 'em is rich, and both on 'em has been good friends to you, or you'd 'a' fared a deal wus than you have," said Ben, not without the hope that, in saying a good word for them, he might say one for himself also.

Clay lay thinking for a moment as his face clouded over, and then brightened again.

"Miss Mercy wouldn't take it, nor the doctor either; but I know who will, and by G—d, I'll do it!" he exclaimed, with sudden energy.

His eye happened to rest on Ben as he spoke, and, feeling sure that he was to be the heir, Ben retired to send Miss Mercy, that the matter might be settled before Clay's mood changed. Miss Carrol came, and began to cut the buttons off Murry's coat while she waited for Clay to speak.

"What's that for?" he asked, restlessly.

"The men want them, and Ben is willing, for the coat is very old and ragged, you see. Murry gave his good one away to a sicker comrade, and took this instead. It was like him—my poor boy!"

"I'd like to speak to you, if you have a minute to spare," began Clay, after a pause, during which he watched her with a wistful, almost tender expression unseen by her.

"I have time; what can I do for you?" Very gentle was Mercy's voice, very pitiful her glance, as she sat down by him, for the change in his manner, and the thought of his approaching death, touched her heart.

Trying to resume his former gruffness, and cold facial expression, Clay said, as he picked nervously at the blanket,

"I've a little property that I put into the care of a friend going North. He's kept it safe; and now, as I'll never want it myself, I'd like to leave it to—" He paused an instant, glanced quickly at Mercy's face, and seeing only womanly compassion there, added with an irrepressible tremble in his voice—"to little Mary."

If he had expected any reward for the act, any comfort for his lonely death-bed, he received both in fullest measure when he saw Mercy's beautiful face flush with surprise and pleasure, her eyes filled with sudden tears, and heard her cordial voice, as she pressed his hand warmly in her own.

"I wish I could tell you how glad I am for this! I thought you were better than you seemed; I was sure you had both heart and conscience, and that you would repent before you died."

"Repent of what?" he asked, with a startled look.

"Need I tell you?" and her eye went from the empty bed to his face.

"You mean that shot? But it was only fair, after all; we killed each other, and war is nothing but wholesale murder, any way." He spoke easily, but his eyes were full of trouble, and other words seemed to tremble on his lips.

Leaning nearer, Mercy whispered in his ear,

"I mean the other murder, which you would have committed when you poisoned the cup of water he offered you, his enemy."

Every vestige of color faded out of Clay's thin face, and his haggard eyes seemed fascinated by some spectre opposite, as he muttered slowly,

"How do you know?"

"I saw you;" and she told him all the truth.

A look of intense relief passed over Clay's countenance, and the remorseful shadow lifted as he murmured brokenly,

"Thank God, I didn't kill him! Now, dying isn't so hard; now I can have a little peace."

Neither spoke for several minutes; Mercy had no words for such a time, and Clay forgot her presence as the tears dropped from between the wasted fingers spread before his face.

Presently he looked up, saying eagerly, as if his fluttering breath and rapidly failing strength warned him of approaching death.

"Will you write down a few words for me, so Mary can have the money? She needn't know any thing about me, only that I was one to whom Murry was kind, and so I gave her all I had."

"I'll get my pen and paper; rest, now, my poor fellow," said Mercy, wiping the unheeded tears away for him.

"How good it seems to hear you speak so to me! How can you do it?" he whispered, with such grateful wonder in his dim eyes that Mercy's heart smote her for the past.

"I do it for Murry's sake, and because I sincerely pity you."

Timidly turning his lips to that kind hand, he kissed it, and then hid his face in his pillow. When Mercy returned, she observed that there were but seven tarnished buttons where she had left eight. She guessed who had taken it, but said nothing, and endeavored to render poor Clay's last hours as happy as sympathy and care could make them. The letter and will were prepared as well as they could be, and none too soon; for, as if that secret was the burden that bound Clay's spirit to the shattered body, no sooner was it lifted off, than the diviner part seemed ready to be gone.

"You'll stay with me; you'll help me die; and—oh, if I dared to ask it, I'd beg you to kiss me once when I am dead, as you did Murry. I think I could rest then, and be fitter to meet him, if the Lord lets me," he cried imploringly, as the last night gathered around him, and the coming change seemed awful to a soul that possessed no inward peace, and no firm hope to lean on through the valley of the shadow.

"I will—I will! Hold fast to me, and believe in the eternal mercy of God," whispered Miss Carrol, with her firm hand in his , her tender face bending over him as the long struggle began.

"Mercy," he murmured, catching that word, and smiling feebly as he repeated it lingeringly. "Mercy! yes, I believe in her; she'll save me, if any one can. Lord, bless and keep her forever and forever."

There was no morning sunshine to gladden his dim eyes as they looked their last, but the pale glimmer of the lamp shone full on the blue and the grey coats hanging side by side. As if the sight recalled that other death-bed, that last act of brotherly love and pardon, Clay rose up in his bed, and, while one hand clutched the button hidden in his breast, the other was outstretched toward the empty bed, as his last breath parted in a cry of remorseful longing.

"I will! I will! Forgive me, Murry, and let me say good-by!"

The Last of Seven

Louise Chandler Moulton

It was a mild, patient face—a face which told the story of long and weary years. The lines on it were the slow chiseling of time—a monumental inscription of all the woman had done and suffered. And not many sadder epitaphs are ever written than that which was traced on the quiet yet rugged features within the framing of that silver hair.

The woman had been young and hopeful forty years ago; so loving, and, she had thought, so loved. Perhaps she *had* been loved, then. Sometimes, out of natures as hard and cruel as the granite rock, blossoms a summer longsome little flower — the one sweetness of a hard lifetime. Such, it may be, was Adam Gibson's love in the brief wooing-time before Rachel Gray, with her bright young beauty, her voice clear and merry as a wild bird's note, and her loving, earnest woman's heart, stood beside him at the altar of the little village church, and then went home with him, his wife.

For the blossoming of that flower of love, for the fond caresses and tender words of that wooing, she would forgive him much, and love him long—love him, indeed, until her tried and patient heart should be done with throbbing to earth's pain and passion.

At the first she had such faith in him. When their short honey-moon was over, and his true character began to develop itself—when she was forced to see that to his hard, worldly nature nothing save his own worldly success was truly dear—when fond lover changed to stern taskmaster, and her burden was laid, almost too heavily to be borne, on her slender shoulders, she fought resolutely against the truth; at least she would not believe him harder or sterner than other men. She said to herself that it was his New England rearing which was in fault—it was because he had been educated to suppress emotion, and to believe in work as the sole business of life. She blamed herself for oversensitiveness; and when, a while before her first baby came, she broke down utterly, and had to steal away to her chamber and give up her tasks to the strong hands of a hired substitute, she sat there through the days of waiting, and meekly pitied her husband because he had married a wife so little suited to his needs, so different from the hardy, long-enduring women around her. She did not blame him for leaving her to her solitude—he had so much to do, she knew, and of course that still room must be wearisome to him. Yet bitter tears fell now and then on the soft muslin fabric of her wedding dress, which she was fashioning into dainty baby robes, her gift to the unborn darling for whose coming she waited in tremulous expectation.

Oh what hopes fluttered at her heart, sweetening the bitterness of her tears! How she forgot all present sorrow in fond dreams of the soft hands that would by-and-by touch her cheek, the little head that would lie on her bosom, the young, innocent lips that should sometime bless her ear with all the words of love for which she hungered!

And when at last the hour came, and through the closed lips fluttered no breath; when she knew that the little dark-lashed eyes could never open, or the little breast stir from its marble slumber, she could not help it if moonless and starless night settled down upon her heart. If Adam Gibson had but loved her and comforted her then—been pitying, and gentle, and tender—he might have won her, body and soul, for his bond-slave forever. But when he stood aloof, looked coldly on her bitter woe, and blamed her excessive indulgence in her sorrow, he roused that meek-

est of natures to revolt. She could forgive him that he had been too busy
with the cares of life to be tender of her, but she could not forgive him that
he did not mourn for his dead baby; and so a bitter seed sprang up in her
heart. She did not cease to love him—she was too loyal a soul to admit the
possibility of that, but she ceased to excuse him or to worship him; before
his altar she burnt no more incense.

And yet she did not quite, in that one matter, do him justice. Under
the hard crust of his nature there was a fountain of tenderness of whose
hidden gleam she never knew. Perhaps there lives no man so hard that the
sight of his own dead child would not move him; and even Adam Gibson
looked upon his with a throb of unconfessed anguish. But he hid his feel-
ings under an iron mask. It was only when no human eye saw him that he
stole, just once, into the darkened parlor where they had laid the dead darling, and touched its tiny morsels of hands, and kissed its little, white,
piteous face with a dumb sense of loss keener than any thing he had ever
felt before.

But he said no word of sorrow, or sympathy, or consolation to the
poor young wife, wrestling alone with the bitterness of her heart-break. He
only told her that it was sinful to rebel against God's will; and if she "took
on" so when she was sick, she would not be likely to get well very soon.
And she thought, with something more like scorn than her gentle nature
had ever felt before, that he was in a hurry to have her get well because he
was unwilling to pay for hired service any longer. From excusing him for every
thing, she had gone to the other extreme, and did him less than justice; for,
apart from all economical considerations, he really had a strong desire to see her
well; to have her face—that young, pretty face—opposite him again at his
meals, and when he sat down at nightfall. Alas! it would never again be the
bright face it had been when he brought it there a year ago.

She got well in time—the lonely, disappointed little thing—went again
about her household tasks, sadder and less trustful than before, but still
gentle. It was then, so long ago, that meek endurance began to write its
lines upon her face. She did not grow feeble or helpless, however. Her

cares and burdens served to develop in her new powers of endurance. She grew efficient; fell into the ordinary routine of the hard-working New England farmer's wife of forty years ago; less angular, perhaps; less self-asserting than most; less roughened by the rough details of her life; soft-spoken and meek-spirited, as stronger neighbors used to call her.

Other children came to her after that; but for nearly twenty years none of them lived much beyond babyhood. Somehow she never expected they would. That first loss she had accepted as a prophecy of her destiny. If that first child—so loved, so waited for—had not found its love and welcome strong enough to hold it back from the land of the angels, how was any other to be wiled into staying with her? I do not think she ever tasted again quite the bitterness of that first grief, though over five more little graves, side by side with the first one, white snows of winter fell and summer wild-flowers blossomed.

At last, when she was nearly forty years old, and had been more than twenty years a wife, her seventh child came. By some singular presentiment she felt, when she looked at it, that this child would live. She did not read in its eyes the shadow of coming doom, as she had in those of the others. She felt her heart quicken into a sudden tumult of rapture as she held the little one to her bosom, and thanked God for this comfort for her old age!

Superstitious crones talked of the luck of odd numbers, and the peculiar luck attending always a seventh child; and it truly seemed as if all the fairies had brought good gifts to the little one's christening. Her mother named her Winifred, after her own mother, dead and gone. Adam Gibson did not interfere. He had grown used, so it seemed, to births and burials, and he let his timid wife have quite her own way with the blossoms that slept such brief while upon her bosom.

Contrary to his expectations, but in accordance with the belief the mother had all along cherished, the little Winifred grew up toward her girlhood as bright and winsome a child as ever gladdened any household.

There was something in the sight of the wee little figure toddling round, under every body's feet, yet never in the way—something in the sound of the clear-piping little voice calling him father, that stirred Adam Gibson's heart as it had never been stirred before, unless it were in that long-past and half-forgotten summer when his love for the child's mother had blossomed, and spent its lavish sweetness on the summer aire, and with the autumn died, as it seemed, like all its summer sisters. Yet, despite his love for his child—a love stronger and more deeply inwoven in his nature than he knew—there was, almost from the first, a sort of antagonism between him and the little one. She was a bright, resolute, willful sprite, with a temper as dominant as his own looking out of her large, wide-opened eyes. To her mother's gentle sway she always yielded instant obedience: indeed, there was something curiously soothing and protecting in her manner toward her almost from babyhood. No one must sit in mother's chair, no one must gather mother's flowers, or interfere with any of mother's comforts; and her very manner of obedience seemed to say:

"Surely I'll do it if you wish. You shall have it all your own way, poor dear. I wouldn't cross you for the world."

But she never seemed to recognize her father's right to command her. He tried to punish her once or twice, but was met, for the first time in his life, by remonstrance from his wife, so passionate that he was startled into abandoning his purpose, and for the most part giving up all efforts to interfere with her gentle government.

The child loved him dearly too, but not at all in the way she loved her mother. She took such liberties with him as no one would have thought he would have endured for a moment, and he found that he rather liked her merry teasing. Still there was an uneasy consciousness in his heart that he was not her master—that her will had never bent itself to his—which deepened as she grew toward womanhood, and kept alive, despite of tender love, that subtle antagonism which would break out by-and-by, perhaps, into tyranny on one side, and revolt on the other.

It was a better sight than most pictures to see Winnie Gibson when she was eighteen. She was taller and more fully developed than her mother had ever been, yet with all her mother's flower-like delicacy. Her large, fearless, innocent eyes had a power in them which never had looked out of Rachel's. It would not be easy to quell that spirit, or break down that resolute will. Her mother had thought often how strong the girl's will was, with restless anxiety, and a secret self-blame, because she had not striven, when she was younger, to break it; as if there had ever been a time since the bairn was old enough to say Mother when she had not been queen and Rachel helplessly subject.

She heard a gush of song outside one summer afternoon, as she sat thinking, as usual, about Winnie, and lamenting her own easy rule. She could not help a smile of pride as she listened to the full, rich voice—a smile which deepened as the girl came in, brightening the room with her glad, young beauty. She walked about for a few moments, putting things to rights a little, with a curious fidgeting air quite unusual to her. Then suddenly she came and knelt down at her mother's side.

"Do you love me much?" she asked, coaxingly.

"You know that as well as I do, darling."

"Will you miss me, then, when I am gone?"

"Gone!" A sudden dismay struck to Rachel Gibson's heart, and made her cheek pale. She remembered six graves: were the angels going to call for this child also?

"Yes, gone, mother darling! I have promised this afternoon to leave you some time—to go away with James Ransom."

"Go away with James Ransom!" the mother repeated after her, slowly, aghast with dismay. "Child, are you mad? Your father will never let you—never. Don't you know that he hates old John Ransom with a life-long hatred? Don't you know that Adam Gibson never changes, never forgives?"

"I don't know that James Ransom is any worse because he is John Ransom's son. As for father, if you think he won't let me marry James, why, I think I won't ask him."

The worst side of the girl's nature was uppermost then. A fierce fire blazed in her eyes, which made you think of some wild creature at bay. Her mother was completely overpowered; her feeble resistance, her weak power of self-assertion, all swept away, as when some impetuous stream overflows its banks and scatters ruin and wreck over peaceful homes. It was just as well, perhaps, that she sat in such dumb silence, for any words would but have kindled Winifred's passion to fiercer heat.

After a while the girl was frightened. She thought her mother seemed as if she were turning to stone. She began to chafe her hands and kiss her, in an agony of remorseful love and sorrow.

"Don't, mother," she cried; "don't look so. Only speak to me. I will not go against my father any more than I can help: only, if there is nothing to be said against James, it would not be right for me to give him up just because my father and his don't like each other."

"You must let me tell him to-night, Winnie, and see what he says. Until after that don't let us talk about it. It frightens me. Sit down here beside me, and let me forget the bad news a while, and think you are my own little Winnie, that used to love me so."

"That *does* love you so, mother," whispered the girl, with soothing fondness: "that would die before any one should harm one hair of your head."

The next morning Winnie's eyes sought her mother's face anxiously. She could gather from it little hope. Rachel was pale and silent. Adam Gibson, too, ate his breakfast without an unnecessary word; and Winnie did not run after him, as he went out to his farm, with any kisses, or merry, teasing ways, as her wont was. The spell of silence seemed to have fallen on her also. She helped her mother quietly to clear away the breakfast things and do up the morning's work, and not till the two had sat down together in the still house did she ask a question. Then it came, anxiously, pleadingly:

"What did father say? Are you *never* going to tell me, mother?"

"It is no use, Winnie. You must give it up. He will never consent—never."

"Give it up!" A smile, just touched with scornful pity, flickered across Winnie's lips. "You don't understand what you say. I could no sooner give up James Ransom than you could give me up, mother. I love him."

Blank terror whitened for a moment Rachel's face, and looked out of her sad eyes. Then all grew dark, and her head fell back against the cushions of her chair, in a dead faint. Winnie sprang to her side, and tried half a dozen simple means of restoration, trembling herself with fear for the consequences of what she had done.

The swoon did not last long. Very soon the mother opened her eyes, and said, faintly,

"It was nothing. I shall be better in a moment."

When she was sitting up again, and Winnie was kneeling beside her, begging her forgiveness with the quick, impulsive penitence of her passionate nature, she brushed back the girl's brown hair with a tender touch, as she said,

"I never yet had any thing to forgive in you, Winnie. Ever since I have had you, you have been good to me. I do not blame you for this. You could not help loving him, I suppose; and there seems no justice in asking you to give him up because your father and his can't agree. Still, it's a dreadful thing to go right against your father's will. It will separate you from me; for I don't think he would ever let you come into the house again."

"Nothing can truly separate us, mother, for we shall always love each other."

"Ay! but what should I do without you all the long days? For eighteen years you have never been one day away from me. How could I live in this still house and never hear you laugh or speak, or see your face, or have kiss or smile from your lips? Oh, child, child!"

Winnie's dark eyes swam in tears. She drew her mother's head to her bosom with the old air of protection which had been so ludicrous when she was a little toddling thing.

"There! don't grieve," she said, soothingly; "I will stay with you, at least for a while. I am only eighteen now. When I am twenty-one I shall have a legal right to take my own course. Till then I will obey my father. So cheer up, darling! you are sure of me for three years. This afternoon I will see James and tell him so."

"But I shall be keeping you from happiness, and your heart won't be here even if you are."

"Yes, it will, mother; you shall find no change in me. It is best to do it. Since father opposes me, I ought not to resist him till I am older. We are young, James and I, and we can afford a little waiting."

That night, just at twilight, Winifred came in, a strange look upon her face—a light in her eyes proud but sad. She did not speak, for her father sat at the table. She waited until something called her mother into the next room. Then she followed her.

"I have told James, mother, and he is going to enlist for the next three years. So we will be happy together as we used to be, you and I. The poor boy will be out of the way."

"But if you lose him! If he should be killed!"

"He will *not* be, mother! I am not bad enough to need such discipline. The great Father pities his children, and he will let me have James back again in safety. I shall not allow myself to fear. I am glad he is going. I shall love him better, and be prouder of him all my life, for doing this work for his country."

"Did you tell the girl what I said?" Adam Gibson asked, gruffly, in his own room with his wife that night.

"Not all. I told her that you would never consent, and she has told him. He is going to enlist for three years. He will be out of your way; but I warn you if he dies it will kill Winnie."

"Girls don't die so easy—or didn't when I was young. Don't worry. Before the three years are out we shall have her married off to somebody better worth having."

Rachel did not contradict him, but she wondered that he did not understand better the steadfast, persistent nature inherited from his own. The very same element of character which made it impossible for him to forgive John Ransom would make it impossible for his daughter to cease from loving John Ransom's son.

That was the fall of '61. Men had begun to find the Great Rebellion a

very real and earnest thing, and were rising up to crush it; making preparations on a very different scale from what they had at first imagined
would be necessary. The regiment which James Ransom joined belonged
to the Army of the Potomac, and was destined to see some of the fiercest
fighting of the war.

Winnie had promised that her mother should find no change in her.
But she could not quite make good of her words. There was no diminu-
tion of affection, indeed; no lack of the tender thoughtfulness with
which—seeming even from childhood to understand all the untold sorrow
of her mother's lot—she had always striven to lighten her burdens. But the
merry girl, full of song and frolic and the exuberant life of youth, was
gone; and, in her stead, an anxious woman moved silently around the
house, making no complaints, saying nothing of her hopes and fears, but
studying newspapers, shivering at rumors of battles, and gentle with a sad,
pitiful gentleness more pathetic than words.

Adam Gibson never once mentioned to his child the name of James
Ransom, but he tried hard to be kind to her in his own way. He bought her
handsome clothes, which she never wore; gave her money, which went all
of it to buy comforts for soldiers far away, or their bereaved wives and children at home; sometimes tried to provoke her to her old manner of teasing playfulness, but never succeeded. She was perfectly respectful to him,
more obedient than she had ever been before; but, beyond the formal kiss
at night and morning, when her cold lips just touched his cheek, never
affectionate. I think that hard, unyeilding heart of his grew hungry, sometimes, to see her as she used to be. Perhaps he repented himself of what
he had done; but if so, he made no sign.

So the years went on. James Ransom never came home, and no one
ever talked about him in the house of Adam Gibson. Once or twice Rachel
had tried to speak some comforting word about him to her child; but the
pale pain of Winnie's face, the stillness of her unresponsive lips, had
silenced her. Whether the girl ever heard of him no one knew; if she did,
she kept her own secrets.

In the early spring of '64 nearly all his regiment re-enlisted, and were home on furlough; but James Ransom was not among them. Rachel guessed by this that he expected to claim his bride in the fall, and was not ready to postpone it any longer. So far Winnie's belief in his safety had been justified. He had had, they heard through village rumor, a few slight wounds, never any thing serious—and he had been in all the battles.

With the commencement of the campaign of '64 would come a new trial, the last and fiercest. Even Winifred, knowing what lay before the gallant army marching on in the way thrice soaked in vain already with the most precious blood of the country, even she lost something of her faith, and grew so weak with fear that the sudden rustle of a paper, or the swift flight of a bird across a window, would unnerve her.

She was standing by the table one day in May, doing some of her customary household tasks, when her father came in. Whether he had taken her silence with regard to James Ransom for the silence of forgetfulness, or whether he was urged on by some fierce impulse to let her know at once that all her hopes were over, I know not. At any rate, addressing his wife, but looking straight at Winifred, he said,

"Mother, James Ransom is dead. He was killed in the battle of the 12th of May."

As silently and helplessly as if she had been shot through the heart Winnie fell to the floor. Her mother sprang to her side, but paused an instant, even before she lifted up the dear head, to utter her cry of indignation:

"How dare you, Adam Gibson, to say the Lord's Prayer night and morning, and ask God to forgive you as you forgive those who trespass against you? Do you want to be forgiven as you have forgiven John Ransom? You are a hard man; you have been hard to me for forty years, and I have borne it in silence; but if you have killed my child, may God forgive you, for I can not!"

He was stricken to silence—partly, perhaps, by his own terror at what he had done, and still more by the fierce wrath of the meek-spirited woman, who had been to him for forty years the embodiment of silent submission and long-suffering. He stood by without a word while she loosened the girl's dress, and bathed her forehead, and chafed her hands. Then he lifted her up tenderly as if she had been an infant, and carried her in his arms to her own room.

She was not dead, for her pulses stirred languidly, and her breath feebly came and went; but she took no nourishment, spoke no word, made no answer, even when her mother called her name.

So she lay for three weary days and nights, with her mother's mild, patient face bending, full of anguish, over her pillow. In those days years seemed to have done their work on Adam Gibson. He grew gray and old, and his wiry figure seemed to bend like a tree before some sudden blast.

The fourth day he came in from some errand which had taken him to the village, with a look of strange excitement replacing the blank despair of his face. He beckoned his wife from the room where she kept vigil beside Winifred.

"Mother," he said, hoarsely, "he is not dead after all. That first report was false. He was wounded and taken prisoner, and now he has been exchanged with a number more of the wounded. They say he won't die, and John Ransom is going on to bring him home. They are giving furloughs to those of the wounded who can bear to be moved, because the hospitals are so full that they'll get better care at home. Will his coming save Winnie's life?"

"What is the use of his coming home, or of saving Winnie's life, when you've set your will up that she sha'n't have him? Better let them both die. Maybe they'll come together in heaven; for it's my belief that the Heavenly Father is kinder than earthly ones are."

"But I am *not* set against them, mother—not now. Your words went home, Rachel—went home. I am a humbled man, and I am willing to give in. I will ask John Ransom to forgive me, and let me go with him to bring his boy back. Only tell me, will it be in time to save our girl's life?"

"God grant it may be!" Yes, it *will* be—it *must* be!" she answered, growing strangely pitiful toward him, now that she saw what a work his grief was doing in breaking down old prejudices, and softening the heart which so many unforgiving years had hardened. She went in then to Winnie, he following. She scarcely hoped to rouse her, but she would make the effort. She bent over the pillow.

"Winnie, Winnie darling, it was not true. It was a mistake. James is not dead, and father is going for him to bring him home to you."

As if fraught with some strange power of penetrating the dulled senses, the life-giving words went home. A smile, wan and faint, but oh! so full of sweetness, flickered across the pale lips, and then they moved, and formed rather than articulated the word "father."

Adam Gibson bent over her, shaken by such a tempest of emotion as he had never known before—a passion of love, and remorse, and hope. He felt her lips touch his face, the first voluntary caress she had given him since he refused to sanction her love: felt it, and then went away to weep, where no human eyes saw him, such tears as he had never wept before; a rain that would soften his heart and make it meet soil for the seeds of hope, and love, and faith.

When he had regained at last his self-control he went up the road that led to John Ransom's house. He found his old enemy in the yard, making some arrangements for his journey. There, under the May sky, with God's peace in the world around them, he went up to John Ransom and put out his hand.

"Forgive me, neighbor. I have been your enemy more than forty years, and called myself your fellow-Christian all the time. Is it too late now for us to begin to be friends?"

His outstretched hand was grasped, and kindness begat kindness, and penitence was the father of penitence. All past faults on both sides were confessed and forgiven; and then Adam Gibson told the story of his child's love and suffering, and asked the question, to him so momentous:

"May I go with you, neighbor, to bring James back? I think I could help you, and I should feel easier if I was doing something for Winnie to make up for the past."

His offer was not rejected, and that very afternoon the two men started to bring Winifred's hero home.

As for her, hope had seemed to penetrate all her veins like an elixir of life. She grew better rapidly, and before the week of their absence was over some pale roses began to bloom on her thin cheeks.

At last they came. The soldier's wound was less severe than they had feared; but, as he was not fit for duty, they had not found it difficult to get for him leave of absence. He came at once to Adam Gibson's house. Even his father was ready to admit that she who had so nearly died for him had the first claim. Triumphantly her father led him in—led him to the easy-chair where Winifred sat, too weak to rise even yet. He put their hands together, and said, fervently:

"I give him to you, and you to him, and I pray God to bless you both."

He heard, as he turned away, her low cry of content—"Oh James! James!"—and perhaps it was the happiest moment he had ever known.

He went out into the other room. John Ransom had gone away to prepare his wife for their boy's home-coming, and Rachel sat there alone. For a moment he looked at her searchingly. With his sight sharpened by self-knowledge, he could read the sad lines which the years had graven on her face. He remembered the bright fresh beauty he had wooed and won; and the old love—not dead all this time, but sleeping—stirred again to the life of youth in his heart. He went to her side and took her hand, making her look at him as he spoke:

"You said I was a hard man, Rachel; that I had been hard to you for forty years; and you said the truth. But our child will live: I have not killed her, and so I may ask you to forgive me. I have not been worthy of your love; but oh! tell me, if you can, that I have not lost it; for never, not even that summer when I won you, did I love you so well as now, my wife, my Rachel!"

She could not speak, but what need of words? Her worn face blushed and brightened with a beauty tenderer than her youth's; her arms—those tired arms, so long empty—fell round his neck; and the lonely heart hushed the throbs of its life-long aching in the rest, won so late, but won at last.

Louisa May Alcott (1832-1888)

Born in Pennsylvania and educated at home, Alcott lived most of her life in Concord, Massachusetts. She turned to writing to support herself and her family after the utopian schemes of her father failed. In her teens she wrote melodramatic newspaper serials. Alcott served as a nurse in Northern hospital during the Civil War. The experience wrecked her health but rewarded her with fame and fortune. *Hospital Sketches* (1863), based on that experience, became a best-seller and gave her time to write *Little Women* (1867), one of the all-time most popular American novels. Every book after that was an immediate success. Alcott died in 1888 on the morning of her father's funeral.

Rose Terry Cooke (1837-1892)

Born in Harford, Connecticut, Cooke was the daughter of a Congressman who took her as a child on political visits to constituents. Bedridden by an early illness, she learned to read at the age of three and graduated from Hartford Female Seminary in 1843. A steady stream of her poems and short stories appeared in such magazines as *Harper's* and the *Atlantic Monthly*, and later in books—*Somebody's Neighbor* and *The Sphinx's Children*. A severe case of pneumonia halted her writing career, and she died in 1892.

Sarah B. Cooper (1835-1896)

Born and educated in Cazenovia, New York, Cooper worked for a year as governess on a Georgia plantation. She then married her Cazenovia sweetheart, Halsey Fenimore Cooper, who was editing the *Chattanooga Advertiser*. Because of Mrs. Cooper's poor health, the family moved to San Francisco in 1869. A woman's suffrage advocate, she became a leading figure in kindergarten education and underwent a sensational heresy trial for opposing Presbyterian dogman about infant damnation. Tragedy, unfortunately, was a constant companion. Her mother died when she was five, and she lost three children in infancy. In 1885, her husband committed suicide after losing his job, and in 1896, her surviving daughter, Harriet, killed them both on the night of December 10th by turning on the gas in their apartment.

Louise Chandler Moulton (1835-1908)

Literary critic and noted author of children's books, Moulton led a literary life. Born in Connecticut and educated there, she married journalist and publisher William Moulton shortly after her graduation in 1855. She was only fifteen when her first published work appeared in magazines. Her first book, *This, That, and the Other* (1854), was a collection of those works. She was literary correspondent to the *New York Tribune* and the *Sunday Herald* in the late 1800s. Popular and prolific, she published some twenty well-received books; including many for children.

Elsie Singmaster (1879-1958)

The girl from Gettysburg, Singmaster was born in Pennsylvania a few miles from the little crossroads town where the infamous battle of the Civil War was fought — the subject of her popular novel, *Gettysburg* (1924). She saw that town as a vast area "spread with stories which I could not gather fast enough." She graduated from Radcliffe in 1907, married musician Harold Dewars in 1912, and lived in Gettysburg. Her works include *John Baring's House* (1920) and *A Boy at Gettysburg* (1924).

Bella Z. Spencer (1840-1867)

Spencer is the mystery woman of this collection. She apparently wrote two novels: *Ora, the Lost Wife* and *Right and Wrong*, or it was perhaps called *She Told the Truth at Last*. This later novel was about the Civil War and its posthumous book publication included four short stories: "Woman in the War," "The Prisoner's Child," "Presentiment," and "The Coquette's Fate." Both books were reprinted several times. She may have been a resident of San Francisco at the time of her death.

Elizabeth Stuart Phelps Ward (1844-1911)

This popular author of religious fiction was born in Boston, the daughter of an Andover Theological Seminary professor, and baptized Mary Gray. She was strongly influenced by her mother, Elizabeth Stuart Phelps, who died when her daughter was eight. The child then took her mother's name. When the Civil War erupted, the young man she loved was killed in battle. The shock drove her into seclusion for years and influenced her most famous novel *The Gates Ajar* (1868), a gentle and humane depiction of life after death, typically mixing mysticism with Yankee common sense. Other works included *Burglars in Paradise* (1886) and *Women and Ghosts* (1869).

Edith Wharton (1862-1937)

Born into the high society world of Boston that knew no reason for women to read and write, Wharton was almost entirely self-educated. In 1885, she married Bostonian Edward Wharton. When he became mentally ill, she cared for him alone when her family refused to admit his sickness. In mid-life she began writing. Her first best-seller was *The House of Mirth*. Fame, awards, and success followed. Two novels, *Ethan Frome* (1911), and *The House of Innocence* (1920), won Pulitzer Prizes. Her ghost stories are supernatural classics. In the early 1900s, she moved to Paris and spent the rest of her life abroad. During World War I, she sheltered and fed six hundred refugee orphans, for which she was made a Legion of Honor officer. She was the first woman awarded an honorary doctorate of literature from Yale. She died in 1937 from a stroke and was buried in Versailles.

Other Books and Audiobooks from August House

Civil War Ghosts
Edited by Martin H. Greenberg, Charles G. Waugh,
and Frank D. McSherry, Jr.
Paperback / ISBN 0-87483-173-3

Confederate Battle Stories
Edited by Martin H. Greenberg, Charles G. Waugh,
and Frank D. McSherry, Jr.
Paperback / ISBN 0-87483-191-1

Ghost Stories from the American South
Compiled and edited by W. K. McNeil
Paperback / ISBN 0-935305-84-3

Tales of An October Moon
Four frightening, original stories from New England
Created and performed by Marc Joel Levitt
Audiobook / ISBN 0-87483-209-8

Buried Treasures of the Civil War
W. C. Jameson
Audiobook / ISBN 0-87483-492-9

Half Horse, Half Alligator
A Publishers Weekly Best Audio of the Year
Performed by Bill Mooney
Audiobook / ISBN 0-87483-494-5

A Field Guide to Southern Speech
Charles Nicholson
Paperback / ISBN 0-87483-098-2

August House Publishers P.O. Box 3223 Little Rock, AR 72203
800-284-8784

Donald Davis Books and Audiobooks from August House

See Rock City
A Story Journey through Appalachia
Hardback / ISBN 0-87483-448-1
Paperback / ISBN 0-87483-456-2
Audiobook / ISBN 0-87483-452-X

Listening for the Crack of Dawn
Paperback / ISBN 0-87483-130-X
Audiobook / ISBN 0-87483-147-4

Thirteen Miles from Suncrest
Hardback / ISBN 0-87483-379-5
Paperback / ISBN 0-87483-455-4

Barking at a Fox-Fur Coat
Family stories to keep you laughing into the next generation
Hardback / ISBN 0-87483-140-7
Paperback / ISBN 0-87483-087-7

The Southern Bells
Audiobook / ISBN 0-87483-390-6

Christmas at Grandma's
Audiobook / ISBN 0-87483-391-4

Rainy Weather
Audiobook / ISBN 0-87483-299-3

Uncle Frank Invents the Electron Microphone
Tall Tales full of Appalachian Wit
Audiobook / ISBN 0-87483-300-0

August House Publishers P.O. Box 3223 Little Rock, AR 72203
800-284-8784